WISH YOU WERE HERE

THE WISHING TREE SERIES, BOOK 3

KAY BRATT

"Bratt writes a beautiful tale of family which grabbed me from the very first page. Quinn, mourning the loss of her mother, must travel to Maui in search of her roots. Leaving behind her fiancé Ethan, she is drawn to the island's rich history and the locals who welcome her into their world. Woven between the pages is the deep mystery of Quinn's past, and the DNA test that leads her to a family she never knew. Bratt takes the reader on a heartfelt journey of family and forgiveness while Quinn teaches us about those we should let in and those we should let go. For at the very core of the novel is the rare gift of being true to one's self." — **Rochelle B. Weinstein, *USA Today* bestselling author**

"*Wish Me Home* has all the trademarks of a Kay Bratt novel: a heartwarming story that nourishes the soul, beloved characters, and a plot that kept me turning pages. Without shying away from the harshness of life, Bratt has managed to create a world in which kindness and goodness prevail. My advice to those who haven't read this book yet? Find your comfy reading spot, get your beverage of choice, and sink into the world of *Wish Me Home*. You'll be glad you did." —**Karen McQuestion, bestselling author of *Hello Love***

"In this inspiring story of a woman's search for the deepest wish of her heart, Bratt paints a realistic portrait of the dark side of the foster care system, while simultaneously reminding us that there is always hope, and that home and family can be found in unexpected places." —**Kerry Anne King, bestselling author of *Closer Home* and *I Wish You Happy***

"With its resilient protagonist, secret that kept me guessing, dog I wish I could adopt in real life, and story that tugged at my heart, Kay Bratt's *Wish Me Home* grabbed me and held me all the way to its heartfelt resolution. Readers who enjoy novels like Vanessa Diffenbaugh's *The Language of Flowers* will find it a delight!" —**Nancy Star, bestselling author of *Sisters One, Two, Three***

"A baring-of-the-soul emotional story that leaves you with a heart full of love and hope." —**Carolyn Brown, *New York Times* bestselling author, for *Dancing with the Sun***

"*In Dancing With the Sun*, a mother and daughter are forced to lean on each other for survival in the wilderness while learning to let go of years of grief and guilt. Readers will relate to Kay Bratt's depiction of a mother's love and her courage in protecting her daughter. Ultimately, though, this novel is a page-turner that will pull on your heartstrings and affirm your faith in humanity." —**Karen McQuestion, bestselling author of *Hello Love***

"*Dancing with the Sun* is an evocative story of emotional and physical survival in the harshest of terrains. Mother and wife Sadie Harlan is struggling silently with grief when she and her daughter go missing in Yosemite. Away from the world and focused on keeping her daughter alive, Sadie embarks on an unforgettable journey through loss and guilt to find forgiveness, healing, and strength. Book clubs will love the powerful message of this unique novel." —**Barbara Claypole White, bestselling author of *The Perfect Son* and *The Promise Between Us***

"*Dancing with the Sun* is an endearing, emotional tale filled with the perfect mix of poignant family heartaches, unshakable mother-daughter love, and a dose of adventure in a dramatic, vivid setting that will sweep you away until the very last page. Don't miss it." —**Julianne MacLean, *USA Today* bestselling author**

"Whether facing the natural terrors of Yosemite or the internal pains of an unforgiven past, this mother-daughter story is beautifully written and relatable as one woman faces a mother's greatest fear—losing yet another child. Kay Bratt delivers on all levels in this emotional and tense story of loss and resilience." —**Emily Bleeker, Amazon Charts and *Wall Street Journal* bestselling author**

"Nothing like a harrowing, life-threatening, and completely unplanned hike through Yosemite's backcountry to make you face years of grief and guilt head on. Kay Bratt pulls this off masterfully in *Dancing with the Sun*, an emotional mother-daughter tale of love, forgiveness, and renewal. Book clubs will love Bratt's latest!" **—Kerry Lonsdale, Amazon Charts and *Wall Street Journal* bestselling author**

"In *Dancing With The Sun*, Kay Bratt captures a mother-daughter relationship with an authenticity rarely seen in novels. Highly emotional, heartfelt, and bristling with tension on every page, this is a story not easily forgotten." **—Bette Lee Crosby, *USA Today* bestselling author**

"*The Scavenger's Daughters* is the kind of novel I'd love to write, but never could. Simply told but beautifully rendered, the reader is swiftly transported into the hearts and lives of a Chinese family after the Cultural Revolution. Powerful and poignant, this story captures the heart of humanity. This is the kind of book that will get shared by friends and chosen by book clubs. A phenomenal story of life and love." **—Karen McQuestion, bestselling author of *The Long Way Home***

"*No Place Too Far* is Kay Bratt at her best. Free up some time, find somewhere quiet, and dive into this story of Maggie, Quinn, the challenges they face, and the people who love them. Once again, Bratt tackles complex contemporary issues with remarkable agility and compassion, and it's an absolute pleasure to be along for this ride. And because Bratt is a master of location, it's even more of a pleasure when the ride takes place on Maui. For a few brief moments, I forgot all about errands and laundry and the minivan and soaked up Hawaii, in all its glorious heritage and beauty." —**Lea Geller, author of** *Trophy Life*

"*No Place Too Far* is the perfect blend of suspense mixed with a magical setting and characters we care deeply about. I loved Maggie and Quinn and rooted for them until the final page. Kay Bratt is a masterful storyteller, and the story's pacing and descriptions of Maui left me always wanting more. Highly recommended for book clubs!" —**Anita Abriel, international bestselling author of** *The Light After the War*

"For two women who live in paradise, their lives are anything but idyllic. Best friends Quinn and Maggie have spent the past year trying to outrun dangers from their pasts—one a stalker, the other family secrets. But now both pasts have caught up to them, and the two friends will have to decide if they should keep running or stand up and fight. In this page-turning drama, Bratt has created two strong, dynamic female characters who readers will be sure to root for." —**Amanda Prowse, bestselling author of** *The Girl in the Corner*

"In this delicious drama set against the backdrop of paradise, Kay Bratt weaves a suspenseful story about finding the courage to fight for happiness, forgiveness, and love. I delighted in the enchanting descriptions of Maui, and I rooted for the characters as if they were friends." —**Cynthia Ellingsen, bestselling author of *The Lighthouse Keeper*, *for No Place Too Far***

https://kaybratt.com
Facebook: https://www.facebook.com/KayBratt
Twitter: @Kay_Bratt
Instagram: @Kay_Bratt

Published in the United States by Red Thread Publishing
ISBN: 978-1-7363514-4-4
FIRST EDITION
Cover by Elizabeth Mackey Graphic Design

❀ Created with Vellum

For our wonderful readers in My Book Friends

PART I

CHAPTER 1

*H*enry leaned back on the bench and looked at his watch. He only had twenty-five minutes left before he needed to be home. Greta had a doctor's appointment, and he wasn't looking forward to it. The sessions were getting harder each time, so he needed to prepare himself.

He looked up, staring into the grand tree with the heavy branches thick with lush heart-shaped leaves, beseeching someone to come near and make a wish. Any wish would do—something simple or rather hard —just like those whispered when a shooting star soared across the sky or you flipped a coin into a wishing well.

Same concept and Henry had hung a wish there himself, a long time ago when he was young and fresh with passion, his future beckoning to him like a friend. Fate had taken him in another direction, and his wish was all but forgotten.

He looked around and noticed that the town around him bustled busily for a Friday morning. It was a different Linden Falls than the one he'd grown up in.

For one, there were many more opportunities to people watch.

Across the way was the old Burford Theatre he would go to when he was a kid. He had many fond memories of afternoons spent there. His dog would escort him all the way from home and wait for him outside on the sidewalk until the matinee movie was over.

Henry could still see him there, patiently watching the people go by, his loyalty unwavering as he waited for his boy.

Now in the place of the theatre was a gift store with a smoothie shop in the back. Henry had never tasted one of their so-called healthy concoctions and had no desire to. He'd wandered in there only once and stood dumbfounded in front of the menu, reading a list of things to add to your smoothie like flax seed and spirulina, two things he'd never heard of in his whole life.

The things people came up with these days.

He'd stick with his black coffee and an occasional lemonade made at home, of course. Greta used to squeeze real lemons, and that was a drink that would whet your whistle. Now he kept a canister of sugar-free lemonade powder in the pantry. It wasn't wonderful but it probably still beat out anything with seeds in it.

As a matter of fact, a cup of hot, steaming coffee

would sure be nice to have while he rested. Too bad there wasn't time.

A couple walked by him, nodding politely. By the way they were dressed, he'd guess they were on their way up to hike to the famous waterfall just outside town. Henry wished he still had the get-up-and-go to hike around and enjoy nature, but his get-up-and-go had got up and gone many years back now.

Young Roland Pickard walked by, almost hitting the lantern pole before taking his nose out of the book he carried and diverting to the right.

Twenty-one minutes left.

The care nurse was very strict about only being there the one hour she was paid for, and he knew he ought not to be lollygagging around.

He felt an hour was barely time enough for her to feed and bathe Greta, much less help him with any of the dozens of other tasks that now fell on him alone. He was grateful to have her though. Any help at all was a blessing.

When he'd promised his wife he'd see her through her illness, he'd had no idea how hard and draining being her primary caretaker would be.

However, he'd said his vows more than sixty years ago, and he'd meant them. If nothing else, he was a man of his word.

In sickness and in health.

Those words had been a constant mantra in his head for the last few months as Greta berated him for

5

stealing her pack of gum or brushing her hair the wrong direction or for forgetting to feed the cat.

The cat that had been dead for at least fifteen years.

Henry didn't argue with her. He even set out a bowl of cat chow every evening, next to fresh water.

When Greta went to sleep, he emptied it so that she'd be satisfied in the morning that Oscar was eating.

Nineteen more minutes.

It would only take seven to walk home. That left him twelve minutes.

He closed his eyes and breathed in the scent of spring, bracing himself for the next few hours before putting Greta to bed.

The weather was just turning warm, and they might even get another cold freeze if the circumstances were right, but Henry prayed they didn't. His hope was that leaving the gray days of winter behind would help Greta to feel more like herself, instead of the combative stranger that now occupied her body. He missed his wife.

Sixteen minutes.

His next deep breath felt like swallowing a stone.

He'd planned to take the hour away to go pay the utility bill and stop by the grocery mart to pick up some fresh bread. Oh, and the sweet milk that Greta liked with her cookies at night. These days if she didn't get her snacks when she wanted them, or forgot she'd already had them, it could send her spiraling into a fit that could scare Lucifer from the depths.

But Henry hadn't made it to the store. It would have

to wait until tomorrow. The soft wave of the tree's leaves in the breeze had beckoned to him, and a few minutes of peaceful rest were too hard to resist.

The breeze picked up again and he opened his eyes.

A new note tied to one of the branches on the tree got his attention. He wondered briefly what was written there and who it belonged to. Some of the locals of Linden Falls still believed in the tree's magic or its ability to help their wishes come true. Tourists also came through, after hearing different stories of wishes made and given because of the town's tree. It had become quite famous, though Henry no longer held any faith in it. His wish, written when Greta first started showing signs of being more than just a little forgetful, hadn't done a thing to change the dire direction of her downslide into dementia.

Today was an especially hard morning for him. Only the night before, the town constable had knocked on his door just after midnight. When Henry looked through the pane and saw that he had Greta with him, he'd just about fainted. He thought she'd been sound asleep the last time he'd checked on her and had gone to bed himself.

The secret of her demise that he'd kept so well for the last two years was unraveling and people were finding out.

Greta would be horrified.

He heard someone behind him and looked to see Neva, the owner of the inn and an old friend of theirs.

He waved politely.

7

The relationship between him, Neva, and Greta was a complicated one. Usually, he tried to avoid getting close enough for conversation with her so that the old memories were kept where they belonged.

Buried.

"Henry," Neva called out. "How are you?"

Henry nodded. "Good, good. And you?"

She was coming straight for him. He'd swear she hadn't aged a bit from when she was a young woman. Unlike Greta, Neva had let her hair go completely gray, and unlike most women her age, she wore it long. She only wore a small bit of makeup, but her eyes stood out big and bright as always. Despite her age and her love of baking she was famed for around town, she somehow maintained the willowy figure she'd always had.

He wondered if she realized how gracefully she'd aged.

"I'm well," Neva said, approaching the bench and handing him a cup before settling on the bench beside him with her own.

He smelled through the lid opening and then looked up at her.

"How did you know I was wishing— Well, never mind. Thank you." He took a sip, nearly closing his eyes with ecstasy over the deep dark taste of the coffee.

"You're welcome. I stopped in to get a cup for myself, and for some reason, they handed me two and said one was on the house."

"Well, that worked out," he said.

"Yes, it surely did, didn't it?" Neva said, chuckling. "I'm out to pick up some last-minute bagels from the Cobblestone Bakery to get ready for a rush of visitors. Next to October when they come to see the leaves, this is my busiest month, and I don't make bagels. I focus my efforts on the sweet stuff."

"That's great to hear business is still good," he replied. "I heard the old house was giving you a bit of a fit."

She shrugged.

"I had a few tough months when the plumbing and then the electricity decided to go into menopause, but nothing my meager savings couldn't handle."

"Good," he said. "I also heard that you let Nancy's relatives from the city stay for free while they attended her daughter's wedding."

Neva laughed. "Well, they did have to set up a few portable restrooms, and we did a lot of old-school living with candles and lanterns, but it was fun and most of them couldn't afford lodging anyway."

Henry wasn't surprised at her kindness. Neva thought of everyone in their town as her responsibility. When Nancy had put out feelers for rooms to rent cheap, he figured Neva would step up and do it for free. She had an instinct to care for others.

Linden Falls was lucky to have her.

Henry looked at his watch.

"I know, you need to get back. But I talked to the nurse and she's giving you an extra half hour today."

9

Henry felt his frown lines over his brow. "You did? Where did you see the nurse? Is everything okay?"

Neva reached over and patted his hand.

Henry tried not to show how uncomfortable it made him, but he slowly pulled it away.

"Yes, everything is fine. I actually just came from there."

That got his attention. In all the decades they'd both lived in the town, Neva had never set foot in his home. It was probably the only house in Linden Falls she hadn't been in, but it was an unspoken boundary kept —though they were always cordial to each other in town or when they were at the same events.

He respected the same boundary at the inn.

"Don't look so surprised," she said, chuckling. "Greta needs a friend right now and who better than the best one she ever had?"

"But—"

She put her hand up. "Shush. I've heard about Greta's illness and how, for the most part, you are trying to handle it—and her—all by yourself. I think it's downright ridiculous that you won't reach out for a helping hand."

"Greta doesn't—" Henry started, stammering over how to say what he wanted to without it reflecting bad on his wife.

"Oh, I know all about what Greta wants and doesn't want. You don't need to tell me. But right now, it's not about what she wants. It's about what's best for her.

And someone must make you see what's really going on here, Henry."

"What do you mean?" He felt a tremor of caution. Here Neva had just been to his home for the first time ever, despite living only five minutes from it for decades, and there was something coming he wasn't going to like.

He could feel it.

She looked around and lowered her voice. "I have never really talked much about it, but I took care of my mother for years after she was diagnosed with Alzheimer's."

"I'm sorry to hear that," Henry said.

And he was. He wouldn't wish it on his worst enemy. Seeing the person that you love slowly disappear day by day, into a stranger who doesn't recognize you or the commitment you shared, was harder than anyone could ever imagine.

"I heard about Greta, and I decided I needed to check on her myself. So, I went over there just a bit ago."

She said it so nonchalantly, like it was just a walk in the park. But he was floored.

"How did she react?"

"Fine. She knew who I was and wanted to talk about old times."

He cringed.

"Oh, not those old times, dear. She stuck to reminiscing about the fun we used to have. Before you came along, she and I spent every spare minute together. I think I knew her better than even her own parents did. And as you know now, Greta wasn't always the easiest person to deal with. I got her skinny butt out of so much trouble. Some of it small stuff but there were a few times I really saved her bacon." She laughed.

"I can imagine," Henry said. Greta was still a pistol. Always had been and was even more so now. Back then, once she had decided she wanted him for her own, he hadn't been able to say no, despite an instinctive trepidation that made him wary.

No was never an option for Greta. She was a woman who knew what she wanted and was used to getting it. Trying to defy her would've been like tangling with a mad water buffalo. Their whirlwind courtship had made Henry feel like he was battling a tornado that was Greta. Then before he could get his breath, he was walking down the aisle, wondering how he'd gotten there so fast.

That fire within her that made Greta unique had also made her addictive so many years ago. And volatile, if he were being truthful. The years with her had been anything but dull. Plenty of times he'd threatened to leave her, but that was long ago when they were still fervent and full of the ebb and flow of emotions that tangled between passion and jealousy.

Eventually the raging fires of passion became a burning ember before going completely out, taking a backseat to the more visceral trials of growing old and learning how to live peacefully together. Now they took separate bedrooms and were more like companions than anything else, though Greta was still the boss, and for all these years, he'd been happy to be under her rule.

It made things much simpler.

She had organized their life, professionally and personally. All he'd had to do was show up and stay within the lines.

He'd sometimes wondered if things would've been different if they'd had children. Sometimes he thought he could just hear what the sound of little feet running up and down the halls of their huge old house would sound like.

But Greta hadn't wanted them, acknowledging that she wasn't the motherly type. She preferred to be the center of attention and never wanted to give that up. But despite no children, their home had been filled with friends through the years.

Some couples they'd gotten especially close with, even taking a few of their holidays together. A cruise here and there, and one time a two-week tour of Italy and then another to Africa.

They made plenty of fun memories with people through the years, but none of them got closer to Greta than Neva had been.

Neva probably knew her even better than he did. And the funny thing was, they were so opposite and separated by circumstances now that no one from outside of Linden Falls would ever guess that, once upon a time, Neva was considered the sister that Greta never had.

Where Greta was outspoken, high-maintenance, and always called the shots, Neva was levelheaded and giving, the agreeable part of their friendship that balanced them out.

At least until it all ended.

Henry had always thought that when Neva and Greta parted ways, it was one of the biggest losses of Greta's life. Her only true friend who accepted her for all her flaws and little quirks. And tantrums.

Just gone.

Of course, she'd never admit as much. His wife was much too proud to try to undo any damage, even that which she was responsible for. But over the years, even though they never talked of Neva again, he'd seen Greta scrutinize the inn when they'd walk by it. He'd also seen the expression of melancholy that Greta tried to hide whenever she spotted Neva deep in a friendly conversation, or laughter, with someone at many of the shared events in town.

He always tried to give Greta extra attention during those times. So many people loved Neva and sang her praises about all she did for the town. Greta had never had recognition or accolades of that sort. She was a smart one and had been the reason their party-planning business had been so successful, but it was by being a no-nonsense businesswoman, and those types tended not to keep lifelong friendships like Neva did.

Like the rabbit, Greta had hustled and worked long hours and nonstop during the years in her prime, moving as fast as she could to build their wealth. And like the turtle, Neva had kept a slower pace, enjoying life and her role as the owner of the inn, caring for not only the visitors but also the people of the town. While she would never be classified as wealthy, she seemed to be happy with what she had, and it appeared to be enough.

"Henry?"

"Henry…?"

He finally heard her through the fog of his thoughts. He felt his neck burn with embarrassment and wondered if he, too, was going daft. But no, he was tired. More tired than he'd even thought. And he still had so much to do before Greta started sundowning.

"I'm sorry, what were you saying? I really must be going."

"No, wait," Neva said. "I came to find you because I want to help."

He was confused. "I don't understand."

"Nothing to understand," Neva said, smiling gently. "I had a feeling come to me recently that you might be overwhelmed, and I know that neither of you have any family that you can bring in for help. You also don't want to involve the townspeople. But I proved today that Greta is ready to be my friend again, and I'm ready to accept that."

Henry had forgotten how her smile could light up a room. He hadn't been this close to her in years.

This was just too much.

He shook his head. "Neva, you don't understand. I'm a little shocked, too, but Greta is just having a good day. Tomorrow might be bad and she could dredge up all kinds of old stuff, then show you the door."

He didn't mention the fact that she might have been friendly today because she just didn't even recognize her own old best friend.

"That's fine. If she shows me the door and I can't talk her out of it, I'll go through it. Then I'll come back again the next day. I have two hours every morning and one hour after dinner that I can give you."

"You just told me it's going to be your busiest month coming up."

"Yes, I know I did. But what I didn't tell you is that I'm going to hire someone else to help. For these times that Loretta decides to follow her muse and takes off on me. That will leave me more time to do what I'm passionate about—helping others. And not just the ones paying me for a room and breakfast."

"I can't let you do that," Henry said, though the thought of having more help with Greta was definitely enticing.

"You can and you will. I have experience with this kind of thing, and I can teach you how to make life easier for both of you. Though I'll tell you now, this is just the beginning. It's going to get worse for Greta. And for you. A lot worse. And I can help prepare you for that."

Henry knew her words were true, though he tried not to dwell on the grim future ahead. Tried not to think about just how bad it would get, and how he'd handle it. He thought about how awkward it was the week before when he'd gone into the bank to get Tilly to help him straighten out his account and put a stop on a multitude of online purchases that Greta had made when he'd dared to fall asleep earlier than her and left her up watching the Home Shopping Network.

It had just gutted him to take her cards and put them into the safe, then change the passcode.

He sighed loudly.

One day at a time.

And who knew, maybe something would happen, and they'd be able to turn her prognosis around. Miracles had been known to happen around the world. It wasn't impossible. And why not Linden Falls?

Neva stood there waiting for him to answer. So patient she was. Always had been, but he knew that quality had also brought her pain. And that he was a part of it. But what he didn't know was how she could just put all their history aside and move on as though their past never happened.

He couldn't let her do that. She'd been through enough because of him and Greta. Things he'd never forgive himself for as it was. He didn't need even more to feel responsible for.

"I'm going to get back to the house," he said, standing. "And Neva, I can't tell you how much I appreciate your offer."

"But?"

"But I'm going to have to pass. Greta doesn't want people to see her like this, and I have to respect her wishes."

The sound of a bus braking to a stop had him turn, then watch as a line of young Girl Scouts exited the door, their faces full of smiles and excitement for a day out. He'd bet they would soon be heading his way to get a gander at the tree and probably hang up a wish or two.

"Henry," Neva said softly.

He turned back to her. "Yes?"

"I told you, Greta was fine with me today. Ask the nurse."

He nodded. "I believe that. But like I said, tomorrow could and probably will be different. Not to mention that it's unfair of me to put that burden on anyone else. She's my wife. And I'll take care of her. On that note, she's got an appointment today and I need to get back. Thank you again, and have a nice day, Neva."

With that he turned and walked away, so he didn't see her response.

His feet felt like lead, but his heart was strong. He didn't want to hurt Neva's feelings any more than he already had, but no one could ever say that Henry W. Harmon the third didn't fulfill his obligations. And without prodding, too.

Greta needed him.

And by golly, he'd be there for her until he couldn't take another step.

CHAPTER 2

*T*wo excruciating hours later, Henry finally convinced Greta she wasn't going to drive. Now she sat quietly in the passenger seat, staring out the window. She had quieted once he found an oldies channel on their satellite radio.

Now she tapped to the beat, her long nails clacking against the armrest.

Suddenly she stopped and turned to him, looking like a small child asking for a treat.

"I can drive tomorrow, though, right?"

He turned the music down a bit. "No, Greta. You can't drive tomorrow."

"You can't tell me what to do, Henry." Now a sullen teenager.

She was right. He'd never been able to tell her what to do.

"The Department of Transportation suspended

your license, Greta. If you drive now, they'll take you to jail."

She looked aghast.

"What in heaven's name are you talking about? I've never even had a speeding ticket."

They had ten more miles until they arrived at the clinic, and it couldn't come fast enough. After her first appointment, she had a biopsy scheduled just down the hall in the other wing.

Henry didn't want her to get into a mood. But he also had to be firm when it came to the things that could hurt her.

"Remember the accident you had a few months ago? When you were going the wrong way down the one-way street in town? You could've killed those people, Greta. Unless your doctor will write a release, you aren't allowed back behind the wheel."

She let out a sigh that could've won an Emmy, then flounced back against the seat, crossing her arms over her ample chest defiantly. "I'm going to have that doctor x-ray your head, Henry. You've lost it if you think I'm going to take responsibility for your accident."

He sighed. "I wasn't there, Greta. You took the keys and left while I was in the shower. You told the policeman you were going to your mother's house."

Greta laughed harshly. It didn't look good on her made-up face. Her lined lips looked clownish when she was angry.

"Now I know you're crazy. Mama's been dead for thirty years."

He glanced at her, surprised. "Yes, she has. I'm glad you remember."

Pleased with his compliment, she took the rest of the trip in silence. But when they turned into the parking lot at the small medical park, she announced that she wasn't going in.

Ignoring her statement, Henry turned off the car and climbed out, shut the door, and went around to her side.

She immediately locked her door and scowled up at him.

He held up the keys and jangled them. "I can unlock the door, Greta. Just open it already. We're going to be late and then they'll bump your appointment down. Do you really want to sit in the waiting room for an hour or more?"

That did it, as he knew it would. Greta was the most impatient patient in the world when it came to waiting for her turn. She worried the front desk staff relentlessly if even five minutes went by her appointment time.

She unlocked the door and he helped her out, then held on to her arm as he guided her toward the clinic entrance.

"I'm not feeble," she said, then jerked her arm free. "I know how to walk. I've been doing it since I was two years old."

Henry chuckled. Anyone listening would wonder why he put up with such a sharp tongue, but he knew that was just Greta. She didn't mean anything by it; she just didn't know any other way. And honestly, he was glad to see her being so spicy—it was when she wasn't herself that he worried the most. If she turned silent, who knew what she could be devising in her imagination.

As luck would have it, as soon as they entered and signed in, a nurse came through the double doors and called Greta's name. She turned and gave him a triumphant smile, then practically danced her way into the back.

Henry followed.

The nurse took her blood pressure (it was normal), her temperature (normal again), then had her stand on the scales. When Greta saw that she'd gained a pound since the last visit, she quickly covered the digital numbers and ordered Henry not to look.

The nurse led them to a room and told them the doctor would be in soon, before she shut the door behind her and disappeared.

While they waited, Greta slipped her bracelet on and off repeatedly, letting it drop onto the stainless-steel countertop and clatter each time.

Henry was about to jump out of his skin when the doctor saved him by coming through the door.

"Well, good morning, Mr. and Mrs. Harmon. How are we doing today?"

"We are doing just fine. But you're late," Greta said, narrowing her eyes.

"We're good," Henry said quickly.

Blessedly, the doctor ignored her jab.

He sat down on his stool, then used his feet to scoot over until he was directly in front of her chair. He read the papers on his clipboard carefully, then looked up at her.

"You still have a bladder infection so I'm going to set you up for an ultrasound," he said.

"You can't just write her another prescription?" Henry asked. It was hard enough to get Greta to come to her usual appointments, and he had a feeling after today, it would be all the harder.

"She's been through three rounds and that's suspicious," the doctor said. "I'd feel better if we look a bit closer."

He wrote something down, then looked at Greta.

"You know the drill, Mrs. Harmon. I'm going to ask you some questions and you tell me what comes to your mind first."

She looked at him with a bored expression. "I'm not a mental patient."

"Greta!" Henry complained. "Please."

She smirked at him.

"Of course you aren't," the doctor said. "If you were, you'd be in a straitjacket. Now, how many toes do you have?"

"Just as many as you do," Greta said.

"Good point. But what's your favorite color?"

"All the colors of the rainbow."

"And what did you have for breakfast, Mrs. Harmon?" he asked.

"Something hot. What did you have?"

Henry's cheeks flamed while the doctor went over to the computer and pecked in some notes. They both knew what Greta was up to, answering the memory questions without really answering at all.

She was sly.

He looked at his notes. "Last visit I noted you were having more back pain than usual. Has that cleared up?"

"No," she said. "It's worse. And this stomach of mine looks like I'm three months pregnant. I'm not eating any more than normal and I don't understand why I'm so bloated."

Henry knew she was really worried about her stomach, considering that she had always been vain about keeping a decent figure.

The doctor nodded comfortingly. "We can prescribe you something for your back, as well as recommend some over-the-counter anti-bloating medication. Try to get more rest." He turned to Henry. "Mr. Harmon, are there any new concerns you want to talk about?"

"Well, she's not getting rest because she won't try to go to bed at a normal time. She keeps me up until I can't stay awake any longer, then she gets up to do something sneaky. She snuck out last night, but she didn't take the car because I've been hiding the keys."

"Damn it, Henry, I knew you hid those keys."

Henry didn't make eye contact.

"Where were you trying to go, Mrs. Harmon?" the doctor asked.

"None of your beeswax." She crossed her arms across her chest.

He looked at Henry pointedly.

"I'm not sure but the constable brought her back when he found her walking around the square in town," Henry said.

The doctor wrote some more notes into the computer.

Greta stuck her tongue out at Henry as the keys clacked loudly.

"I see you have another appointment after this one, Mrs. Harmon. Do you remember what it is?" the doctor asked, looking directly at Greta.

"Of course I do. I'm getting an autopsy."

"A biopsy, Greta. Not an autopsy," Henry said, feeling sweat bead his upper lip. It wasn't as though he wasn't already worried enough that she'd found a lump. Now she was calling it an autopsy, making it sound even more horrifying.

"Confusing words is expected at this stage," the doctor said.

"At this stage of what?" Greta asked, suddenly serious.

The doc backed away from the computer and looked directly at her.

"Mrs. Harmon, as we discussed at your last visit,

you are having substantial loss of memory and cognitive function."

His words brought Greta back to reality and her lip started to quiver.

"I have Alzheimer's, don't I?"

Henry's heart shifted. He hated to see her armor fall and witness her so vulnerable. It was so seldom, but she'd said the exact same words the last time the doctor had talked to her. Was she going to have to live through this moment repeatedly?

The doctor frowned at her. "While there is not a blood test or a brain scan that can tell us conclusively that it is Alzheimer's, we will continue to treat your issues and follow your progress. There are research and ongoing experiments all the time that show promise for a cure in the future."

Henry's head buzzed. The doctor had said the exact same thing the last time. Despite his holding on to hopes for a miracle, they all knew that Greta wasn't going to be around when and if any cure was found. And for some reason, the doctors and nurses were afraid to say the word *Alzheimer's*. He'd peeked at her chart once, and they'd written *dementia*, along with a lot of other complicated terms he didn't understand.

"What's going to happen to me?" Greta said, huge tears running down her face in a trail of black mascara.

Henry went to her and put his arm around her shoulders.

"It will be fine. We'll get through this," he lied.

The doctor cleared his voice. "On your next visit, I

want to talk to you both about beginning to build a care team. I know the state only allows you minimal professional in-house care, and you are going to need more. I'm not sure what your budget allows, but we need to prepare advanced directives."

Henry wouldn't put Greta in a memory care home, so he hoped the doctor wasn't suggesting that route. However, he agreed it was getting harder and harder for him to do most everything himself. He thought of Neva and her offer to help him with Greta.

That was the only care team he could imagine stepping up and he couldn't let her do that.

"Continue on the medication and I'll see you in a month," the doctor said, smiling as he stood and headed for the door.

Henry wanted to stop him. To tell him that while he was going on his merry way to the next patient, Greta was dying, and Henry didn't know how to save her. He didn't even know how to talk to her anymore.

He just wanted his wife back.

But the doctor was gone in a flash and that left him and Greta alone.

She didn't need to see him being weak.

"We need to get on to the next appointment for your biopsy," he said, handing her the handkerchief from his pocket as he strained to keep the sudden panic from his voice.

She nodded as she dabbed her face, giving an unusually meek agreement. He helped her up and she didn't refuse his arm.

They went to the door.

One foot in front of the other.

That's all they could do.

While life as they'd always known it crumbled down around them.

CHAPTER 3

*N*eva was usually of the most organized sort and never cut things close. However, since she'd had to make a run to the grocery store for a can of cherry pie filling that she had no intention of using but felt urgent to have on hand, she was still adding last-minute seasonings to her spaghetti sauce when the doorbell rang.

She washed her hands and, still drying them on her apron, went and opened the door, trying not to look as flustered as she felt. Usually, she was great with new company, but this time, she was a nervous Nellie.

But then seeing the three of them standing there filled her with a surprising amount of joy. Much more so than when she usually had guests arrive, or any of her friends. Her nervousness fluttered up and away. She couldn't wait to get to know them and learn more about why they'd come to Linden Falls.

"Please, come in," she said, standing aside to let them pass.

The girls were obviously happy to be there, but Janie, she still wore that resolute and guarded expression.

Neva kept her attention on the girls, as they welcomed it more than their mother.

"Well, goodness, Breeze, how pretty you look."

Breeze beamed under the cute pigtails. She wore a glittery pink skirt with a purple unicorn top. But her feet were encased in some fairly grimy sandals. Breeze lost her smile when she saw Neva's eyes travel down.

"I need new shoes," she said.

"Join the club," Carly said.

Neva noticed that the big sister wore Converse sneakers that had obviously seen their share of a few bumpy roads. But her clothes were clean, and her hair appeared to be freshly washed. For a teenager, she didn't wear much makeup, a fact that impressed Neva and that was a nod to the girl's intelligence. With her strawberry-blond hair and bright blue eyes, she was quite the natural beauty. It was a shame that so many girls these days hid all their God-given gifts under whatever they could find on the internet to make them look different.

Janie had smartened up right nice. She wore several different shades of earth tones from head to toe in a loose creamy-colored scarf blouse over wide, flowy palazzo pants and wedge heels. Her statement piece of a three-layered necklace with a silver mandala pendant and a dark blue stone in the middle was the perfect touch without being too much.

Neva was quite impressed with her style. It felt so casual, yet elegant, too.

"Well, come on. Let's go in the kitchen so I can get the bread into the oven and top the salad," Neva said.

They followed as she led them down the hall, but Janie stopped at the long line of framed photographs, examining each one before she caught up with them.

Through the parlor they went, and into the kitchen.

Neva beckoned for them to sit at the small table.

"Wow. This is amazing," Carly said, her gaze taking in the room.

"Oh? Is it?" Neva didn't think it was anything special, but she did love the fact that it was a bigger kitchen than the usual ones in homes of the same age.

"It's very quaint," said Janie. "Just what I expected."

"I think that's an accurate description for a home built in 1806. I believe the house was described as grand back in the day, but quaint fits it better now," Neva said.

"What's that?" Breeze popped up from her seat and skipped over to the sink, then bent and looked around the lacy curtain below it. Myster stared out at her, making her recoil with surprise, then let out a long giggle.

Neva laughed. Then she remembered the fairy door. Yes, Breeze was definitely of the sort that would've put that door there at the tree. Something told her not to bring it up for now, that later she would have an idea of the best way to approach it.

"Other than my sneaky cat, Myster, it's what is always below a sink. My can of lard. Cleaning supplies. Gloves. There's always been a curtain in front of it instead of a cupboard door, for some reason. To be honest, when my brother and I were kids, we took turns hiding under there and scaring our cook. I guess Myster took over that job."

Janie looked away. Neva figured she must not like cats and hoped she wasn't allergic or something.

"Speaking of cook, I need to finish up and get you girls fed," Neva added. "Breeze, let Myster stay in there because I don't want him begging from the table. Sometimes he thinks he's a canine instead of a feline."

Breeze gave the cat one last pet, then joined her mom at the table again.

"Ms. Cabot, can I help you with anything?" Carly offered.

"Why, yes, you sure can, sweet girl." She didn't usually like anyone messing around in her kitchen, and especially not her fridge, but with them she felt an unusual comfort. "If you will, take the salad out of the fridge and top it off with some tomato wedges. You are allowed to use a knife, right?'

Carly and Janie both laughed.

"Yes, she knows her way around a kitchen knife," Janie said. "My girls are raised to be independent. I don't hover."

"Great, the tomatoes are in a paper bag in the

pantry. I had to hurry them along to ripen." Neva finished slathering garlic butter on the bread and slid the pan into the oven. Then she quickly added the pasta to the boiling pot of water on the stovetop, set her timer, then leaned against the counter and took a deep breath.

She was tired.

"Are we eating in here?" Breeze asked.

"Well, usually guests eat in the dining room," Neva said, leaving out the part about the kitchen being her private space, the room that held the most memories of her family in her childhood days. She'd already invited them in there—a total surprise moment for her. And now she realized that she also didn't mind if they ate there, too. "But I'll let you decide. If you want to eat in the dining room, take that stack of plates and the silverware in there and set the table."

Breeze looked from Neva to her mother.

Janie shrugged and raised her eyebrows as if it didn't matter to her.

"I want to eat in here," Breeze said. "This room is friendly."

Neva laughed. "I agree. It's always been good to me, too, considering all the history we have together. Okay, so set the table, please."

With the three of them working together, soon they were all gathered around the table and the girls had filled their plates to the brim. Janie had a portion of spaghetti and a slice of toast, too, but for the most part, Neva saw her only picking at her salad. Something was on her mind, that was clear, but perhaps she was worried about the job. She would have to wait for details because it wasn't proper to talk business at the table.

Neva took a long drink of her lemonade.

"I didn't have time for anything fancy, but there's vanilla ice cream in the freezer for dessert." She didn't mention she'd had to bake a few pies and a new pound cake the day before, because those were for the paying guests, and she hadn't had time to do anything extra.

"I love ice cream," said Breeze, and Neva wanted to hug her for her constant positivity.

They all dug in, and between bites, Neva told them about Linden Falls and the people who lived there. The girls were especially interested in Gladys, the town golden retriever who seemed to belong to everyone and hung out on the square.

"Tell us about the Wishing Tree," Breeze urged Neva.

"It's not a magic tree," Carly said, rolling her eyes.

"Then why do people hang wishes on it?"

Neva cleared her voice, interrupting the back-and-forth. "I can't say whether the tree is magic or not, but many think the wishes they've hung there have been granted."

Janie gave a derisive snort. "If that is so, then I should go down there tomorrow and hang a few myself. I'll wish that there was no hate in the world, that chocolate doesn't have calories, and I will win the lottery."

Gently, Neva moved them away from the talk of the tree. She was protective of it and having it spoken of with mockery filled her with sadness.

"Have you been in the Town Square bookstore?" she asked.

"Yes, I took Breeze there while Mom was sleeping," Carly said. "I love it, but we can't afford books right now."

"Then I have a good idea for you," Neva said, winking at Carly. "You and Breeze get yourselves down to the library. They have a wide selection of books. Something for everyone, I'd say."

"They will be going there soon. My girls are big readers," Janie said defensively. "Tell us more about the people here."

Neva liked that she was showing interest in the town after her moment of sarcasm, and she tried to think of fun things to describe about many of her neighbors. When she got around to describing the always curious Calvin and how she had to be careful what she told him or she'd see it in print the next week, she was pleased to even get a snicker out of Janie, who was mostly quiet.

"Sounds like a sitcom around here," she said. "Next you'll tell me you have a noble sheriff and a ridiculous deputy named Barney."

The girls looked confused, and their mom explained quickly, resulting in another eye roll from Carly and a big smile from Breeze.

Neva couldn't quite figure out Janie. Her daughters

were animated and obviously weren't afraid of conversation, but other than a few times when she perked up, Janie was a bit withdrawn.

When they finished, Neva stood and rubbed her hands together.

"Carly, if you'd take over the kitchen and scoop the ice cream, I'd like to talk to your mom about the open position while I show her the rooms. You can catch up or feel free to explore on your own."

CHAPTER 4

*J*ust down the street, Henry stared up at Greta from his place in his armchair. The evening was turning out to be an unusually quiet one, and he'd just been musing about how well his wife had done all day before retiring to her room to watch her recorded daytime shows.

He'd had an hour of nothing but peace and quiet, and it had been pure bliss.

Now she stood towering over him, holding a dress to her middle as it tangled around her waist. Her hair a fright with curlers hanging limply in a few different areas. She'd tried to apply her makeup and it was definitely not up to her usual skill level.

"Can you help me, Henry?"

He noticed she was wearing a fancy bra, too. "What are you doing?"

"Getting ready for the party. Shouldn't you be dressed by now?"

He put the paper down on the side table, sighing heavily.

"We aren't having a party, dear."

Greta pursed her lips together and narrowed her eyes.

"Henry, stop lollygagging around. You know the caterer will be here shortly and you need to light all my candles and help me pick out some soft music. I have last-minute flowers to arrange, on top of a ton of other things to take care of before the guests arrive. If you don't start moving, you'll ruin the Andersons' engagement dinner."

Henry considered his options.

He knew exactly what decade and even what year Greta was visiting in her mind. While most of their party-planning events were held elsewhere, his wife had held some of the more special dinners for close friends and their families at their home, as another way to show off her exquisite talent.

The Andersons had now been married for more than twenty years and had two sons in college. Their party was probably very memorable to Greta because it had almost been the end of the engagement before it had officially started when Ron Anderson was caught having a private conversation with one of his old girlfriends in the pantry. His fiancée had pitched quite the fit before Greta made her realize that it was truly nothing. She'd ended the dinner feeling like a hero.

He remembered Neva's advice.

But did Greta really want to relive the party? Or simply the feeling of appreciation?

He rose and went to the cabinet that held dozens of photo albums. Greta had always chronicled everything in their life, proof to her and probably others that, even without children, they had been happy and successful.

He looked at the spines, thankful that she'd marked them all. She'd always been after him to be more organized. He had tried—oh, how he'd tried.

Organize, don't agonize.

That was Greta's mantra and he had heard it for decades. Who knows? Maybe she was planning for a time such as this when she was going to have to step down from the job as CEO of their life, and he would need to take over.

He'd do anything to have his old Greta back.

"What are you doing, Henry? Help me get this dress up! I think I may have gained weight since I bought it."

"Just a minute," Henry said. Yes, she'd gained thirty years and at least thirty pounds, and that was him being kind, but she was still lovely.

It took two tries because he'd been off by two years, but finally he found the right album. He carried it to the kitchen table and sat down. She followed, as he knew she would, so that she could keep nagging at him.

"Sit down, Greta. I want to show you something." He started flipping through the book.

She rattled on about not having time and how he was getting on her last nerve, but when he didn't look up or react, she sat with a loud thump.

"What?"

He found the page and pushed the book toward her.

"Look. This is you and me at the Andersons' engagement party. You are wearing that dress."

She stared down at the photo and he could see the exact moment that something clicked for her, because she flinched.

"You looked beautiful that night, Greta," he said, softening the blow. "You still do."

Finally, she looked up at him and he had to give her credit, there were no tears. She was holding on tight to the strong part of herself that had weathered her through many storms, but he didn't know how much longer she could hang on.

He closed the book. On the photos and on their past.

"Let me help get you ready for bed," he said, rising from the chair and feeling at least a hundred years old.

She remained silent, lost in thought.

He felt bad for thinking of it, but her quietness was much preferred over how lately she started asking a multitude of questions just when the day was winding down.

The night before, she'd insisted that she had to leave and go check on her parents. He wanted to tell her she'd be traveling across town to the graveyard to do it, but he knew that would've been cruel, so he convinced her they were away on one of their many cruises around the world.

Sometimes it was easier to join her reality rather than try to bring her to his. Tonight, though, he felt strongly that she wouldn't have stopped the charade until she knew she was confused.

He marveled at how much worse she'd gotten just over the last few days.

Carefully, as though escorting her to dinner, he took her arm and helped her from the chair.

She let him lead her to her room and then into the bathroom.

While she stepped out of the dress and let it fall to the floor, he found her favorite soft sleeping gown, and after getting her out of her brassiere, he pulled the nightgown over her head and let it slide down her body.

When she was dressed, he had her sit, then slowly removed the curlers from her hair and used his fingers to brush it down neatly.

"Can you get this stuff off my face?" she asked meekly. She looked exhausted and he couldn't imagine the efforts she'd taken in her mind to try to get her thoughts organized for a party she'd already given long ago. How many mental lists she'd gone over and tasks that she'd reminded herself had to be done.

He would need to talk her into taking one of the little blue pills to help her sleep. But that was a battle to put aside for the moment.

"Of course. I'd be happy to."

Henry found the cream she used every night and

used it on wads of tissue to wipe her face clean. It took more than a few attempts to rid her lips of the dark rouge color. It had been years since he had been so close to her mouth and the memories flooded back. Her sensual and intoxicating smile, teasing him into doing things he knew he shouldn't do that first night together. The way that mouth continued to tantalize him over the years, usually after he was ready to walk out the door and she used it to lure him back into docility.

Now her skin was paper-thin, and her lips were no longer full and luscious, but they still held many secrets. Probably more than he ever needed to know.

She took out her dentures and handed them over and he dropped them in her cup. She'd hidden the teeth for at least a year after she had finally gone through the procedure. He was glad she'd gotten past that nonsense. It wasn't any use to fight the process of aging, as the alternative wasn't something to covet.

A bottle of expensive night serum shined from the countertop, and she reached for it, then handed it to him as if he knew what to do with it. But then, it wasn't rocket science and he spread some across his fingers and gently, while she leaned her head back against his waist, he reached around and worked it into the skin around her eyes and mouth.

"I'm tired, Henry." She rose and went to her bed, standing beside it.

Henry moved around her to pull the satin coverlet back and move her collection of throw pillows to the side. Then he stepped back and waited for her to climb in.

While she was getting herself comfortable, he went back to the bathroom and drew a glass of water and shook a pill out of the bottle. He brought it back to the bedroom, and thankfully, she took it without fuss.

When he'd tucked everything around her, he leaned down and kissed her forehead, letting his lips linger longer than usual.

"Sleep tight, my Greta girl. Tomorrow will be better."

It was a somber moment. One of realization for them both.

Everything was different. And it would never go back.

This was the rest of their life.

"Will you stay while I pray?" Greta asked, taking his hand.

"Of course." Henry perched on the edge of the bed, feeling fatigue wash over him. It was barely seven o'clock and he wanted to sleep, too. He wouldn't mind one of her magic pills, either, if it would make him forget for the night.

Greta clasped his hand to her chest and closed her eyes.

"Now I lay me down to sleep, I pray the Lord my soul to keep. If I should die before I wake..." She paused for far too long and Henry opened one eye.

She squeezed his hand again and he closed it. "I pray he takes me in an earthquake."

Henry's eyes popped open.

Greta burst out laughing. "I forgot the rest, but that's good enough."

He laughed with her. Never at her.

She still had her spunk.

CHAPTER 5

*N*eva took Janie back through the hall and into the parlor. "This is where guests congregate before dinner, and sometimes even after if they don't feel like using the porch or going downtown for a stroll. We also have a sunroom in the back where the cats love to nap and the guests can take their morning tea."

Neva noticed Janie smile slightly, obviously approving of the sunroom.

She took her across the hall.

"And this door leads to my private sitting room." She opened it wide for Janie to see the small, cozy room with its tall wing chairs that flanked the hearth. A stack of books took up residence on the table between them, and the smell of past fires lingered in the air. Neva was most proud of her Aubusson rug that was the focal point of the room. It was a splurge from at least two or three decades past. Other women her age had diamonds, fancy cars, or all manners of luxurious bobbles given to them from loved ones as gifts for anniversaries or birthdays. Neva had no one to spoil her in that way. Then in one out-of-character moment in an antique store she'd visited in New York, she'd decided she had to have it.

Printed in delicate creams and the lightest of blues, the inner border boasted floral sprays and acanthus scrolls, with a trail of musical instruments around the central floral arrangement of delicate flowers.

"Oh my," Janie said after taking in a deep breath. "That rug is amazing."

Neva beamed. She was thrilled that they were on the same page about her favorite piece in the room.

"Thank you. It's even prettier in the mornings when the sun comes through that window and makes a pattern across it."

"Is it a copy?"

"Actually, it isn't," Neva said softly. "I don't normally splurge on things, but I saw it and had to have it for this room."

Janie shook her head in amazement. "Did you know that the origins of these rugs and the tapestries are not really known for sure, but some historians think they were brought to France by members of the Saracen army?"

"Why, no. I didn't know that. How interesting."

"And what's really crazy is that these rugs are still being handmade in the small village of Aubusson, just outside of Paris. More than a thousand years later."

Neva held her hand to her heart. "Now it makes sense why they are so pricey!"

Janie laughed softly and Neva led her out and shut the door.

"Let's head upstairs."

Janie followed quietly, pausing here and there as they went.

"This is the Robert Frost room," she said at the doorway to one of the larger rooms.

"Did he stay here?"

"No, but with our state being such a pull for writers to come and find solace, I renamed all the rooms after famous authors. We also have a Kipling, Stegner, and Galway room up here."

"I don't know any of those," Janie said.

"Galway won a Pulitzer Prize for poetry, and Rudyard Kipling is the author of *The Jungle Book*."

"Oh. Yeah, I know that one."

"That was my brother's room growing up, though Willie died before he could know I renamed it a few years back, in memory of his favorite book."

"Can I see it?" Janie asked.

"Sure—right down here," she said, leading her down the hall. "It's across from the bedroom that used to be mine. The rooms share a bathroom on this end. I stay on the first floor now and only come up when I have to, which has been far too much the last few weeks since Loretta took off."

"Loretta?"

"Oh, she's my flighty housekeeper. That's why I

asked if you'd like to have some work until she returns."

"If she's flighty, why do you keep giving her job back to her?"

"Oh, because she means well, and I like that she lives her life fearlessly. When she thinks she sees an opportunity, she takes it. If it's not the right one, she comes back."

Janie snorted. "Wouldn't we all like to live so freely? She must not have children to protect and provide for."

Neva wasn't sure how to respond to that, so she didn't. To be honest, she wasn't sure where Loretta went to or what she was doing on her little getaways, but when she returned, it was always a joy to have her back in the house again.

Neva stopped at the door to the Kipling room and moved aside so Janie could enter. It was a fine room and the only one that, in previous times, because of its wide expanse of windows that could be opened, allowed cigars. She swore she could still smell the faint aroma of a good Cuban blend.

"Why did you get to keep the inn and not your brother?" Janie asked.

Neva fluttered a hand in the air. "It was his, too, but he didn't want it. Willie was a bit of a beatnik back then and he headed out to the West Coast."

"What's a beatnik?" Janie asked.

"Oh, just means when he came of age, he was philosophical about avoiding materialism, and he was anti-authoritarian. If he'd have taken the inn, it would've been gone the first year. He refused to pay the government their taxes on the property. Our father called it social defiance. He and Willie never got along because my brother wasn't one to follow norms."

"So, he was a hippie?"

Neva laughed. "Not when he left Linden Falls, he wasn't. But by the time he hitched a ride and ended up in the Earth's People's Park in Norton, I guess you could say he went through a phase."

"What is that?" Janie asked. "A commune?"

"No. It wasn't a commune. There wasn't any ideology or anything like that. Just fifty-five acres of land that no one could own, where people came to camp and settle and supposedly live with no rules. A lot of campers and tents. Some ramshackle houses and even some halfway decent homes."

"You saw it?"

Neva smiled. "I sure did. My parents didn't know it, but one weekend when they thought I was away at a girls' camp, my boyfriend took me there to see Willie."

"Did you find him?"

"I sure did. We got there late on a Saturday night and there were a lot of people sitting around a river at the entrance to the park. Cooking, drinking, just having a good time. Willie saw me right when I walked up and just about flipped his lid. He threatened to whoop my boyfriend up one side and down another if he didn't take me straight home and swore that, if anything inappropriate happened along the way, he'd find him and make him wish he'd never met me." She laughed, remembering how upset he was, as though he was her father.

"Sounds like Willie was a rebel," Janie said.

"Oh, not really. He moved on from the People's Park rather quickly and headed to California. Willie was a good guy, and it pained our father that he was more interested in writing and literature than learning a trade he could support a family with. But Willie just liked to be his own person."

"So he disappointed your family." She looked sad.

"No, not all of us. I was glad he had the guts to go off and do what he wanted with his life. He had enough adventures for the both of us and he could've come back at any time. But he was sowing his oats, married and divorced twice before he was thirty-five years old, then a proclaimed rest-of-his-life bachelor."

"You should've hooked him up with Loretta."

Neva laughed. "He was much too old for her."

"And he didn't want his part of the profits of the inn business once he realized it took money to get by in this world?" Janie asked.

"Oh, there isn't much to split, dear girl. I have to give it to him, though. He never asked me to sell and give him half, and I could've, many times. I've had several investors try to buy me out. Willie knew how much this place means to me and would never ask me to do that."

"So, what did he do for a career?"

"No real career. He had an entrepreneurial spirit and was always just on the cusp of the next big thing. It usually burned out fast, but somehow, he always made enough money until the next grand idea. Then again, from what I can gather, he spent any profits as fast as they came in. He was single when he died of a heart attack a few years ago, but I think he left quite a trail of sweethearts up and down the coast. Always was one to lure them in."

Janie continued walking around the room, inspecting every detail. She went to the wall of windows and gazed out, examining the view.

"It's a big room for a child."

"Yes, it was. I was always jealous because mine was smaller, but he said he had to have this side of the house so he could see the moon. I think it had more to do with that easy landing that he'd slide down, then grab a tree to hit the ground and go see his girlfriends, when he was in school. But it's a good size for renting now. It's big but we keep everything fairly clean of clutter so that it makes it easier to clean. Loretta changes the bedding, dusts, and runs the vacuum and is in and out of the rooms in under half an hour each."

"Aren't there hardwoods under this carpet?"

"There are, but they've been covered for a very long time. And they'd need a lot of work."

"It would be worth it," Janie said. She walked around the room, running her hand over the top of the bureau and then along the bottom frame of a painting of a scene in India.

"Kipling was born in India," Neva said.

"But he was English, right?" Janie asked.

"Yes."

"I would design this room with a very faint outdoor theme. Nothing cartoony like *Jungle Book*, but perhaps faux fur rugs and a majestic painting of an elephant on the wall. I'd keep the brown tones in the drapes and the bedding but lighten it up with some ivory trimmings with throw pillows and such." She spoke wistfully.

Neva smiled. "That sounds lovely, dear. I'm sure all the rooms could use a refresh, but to be honest, the budget isn't there. Let me show you the other rooms." She led Janie out and they passed by the other five rooms.

At the end of the hall, Janie stopped at a small door.

"What's this go to?"

"That's the attic entrance. Many years ago—way before I was born—the Irish staff who ran the house stayed up there. It's really just storage now."

"Can I take a peek?" Janie was already opening the door.

"I don't think—"

Too late. Janie was on her way up.

Neva pulled the long string to their right and the bulb at the top came on, lighting their way. Before they were halfway up, the girls were behind them. Janie reached the top first and stopped at an antique dressing table, exclaiming over what it could be with some restoration.

Neva was embarrassed. It had been ages since she'd been up there.

"Carly made dessert," Breeze sang out.

"Ice cream?" Neva asked as she got to the top of the stairs and paused, holding on to the banister as she caught her breath.

Janie went on without her, walking around the attic, peering at framed art stacked against the wall and into trunks randomly strewn about.

Carly joined her while Breeze went around them. "Not just ice cream. I made homemade cherry crisp. I hope you don't mind but I used your only can of cherry pie filling."

Neva smiled at her. "Of course not. How convenient that I had one there waiting. Did you find everything else you needed?"

"I sure did. Just a bit of flour, brown sugar, cinnamon, and allspice for the streusel. And you had plenty of butter. Oh, and I found the lemon juice. It's all in the oven now and needs five more minutes. Then all we have to do is scoop the ice cream beside it."

"Well, I'll be," said Neva. "I'm quite impressed. How old did you say you are?"

"Sixteen. But I've been cooking since I was nine. I'm also teaching myself to speak French so I can apply to go to culinary school in France. *J'ai une faim de loup!*"

"And that is?" Neva raised her eyebrows.

"It means I could eat a horse." Carly laughed.

"I hate cooking," said Breeze from twenty feet away, where she was looking at a long gown that hung wrapped in plastic. "Is this a wedding dress?"

Neva joined them. "It sure is. It belonged to my grandmother and my mother wore it, too."

"Did you wear it?"

"I did not," Neva said. "I never married. It's not that I never had anyone ask, it's just that if I were going to get married, I wanted to be very married. And I never felt that opportunity presented itself. I did, however, wear some of those old ball gowns in a trunk up here somewhere."

Both girls stared at her, and Neva felt uncomfortable at the pity in their eyes at the mention of not being married. It wasn't a nice feeling and it brought unpleasant memories crashing back.

"You know," Janie said, coming close and interrupting the awkward pause, "this is a huge area. It must be at least a thousand square feet or more. You should really think about expanding. A third-floor getaway—maybe a honeymoon studio apartment with all the works. There's a lot you can do up here with this."

Neva chuckled. "Wouldn't that be just as sweet as can be? It's twelve hundred square feet of space. But it would take quite an investment, especially because there's no plumbing up here. If I were going to expand, I'd start with the carriage house because it was outfitted as a dwelling at one time. It has a bath and a half and a bedroom, plus a small loft."

Janie stopped moving around and turned to face her.

"Is the carriage house inhabitable?"

"Well, hmm…not really anymore. It needs a lot of tender loving care before I could ever put guests in it, but so far, I haven't felt the need for more room. Some of the fancier inns outside of town get the most business."

They heard a timer ring out and Breeze clapped her hands.

"Dessert! Can we go downstairs now, Mom?"

Janie looked lost in thought, but she let Breeze take her hand and lead her to the stairwell. Neva and Carly followed.

"I'll get it out, Breeze. Don't touch the oven," Carly said. Under her breath she grumbled about her little sister taking the lead. "You'd think it was her creation instead of mine."

"I just can't wait to try your cherry crisp, Carly," Neva said from behind. "And I'd love to have your recipe. It will be a nice switch up from the apple pies I'm always making for guests. But first, let's hurry before Breeze wishes that stuff out of the oven and eats it all herself."

Neva was enjoying having the company, but she needed to get to bed to be up bright and early, and Janie still hadn't said one word as a hint as to whether she had any interest in the housekeeper position.

Janie was already pulling the cherry crisp out of the oven when Neva and Carly joined them, and Breeze was carrying the box of ice cream over to the counter. Within three minutes they were all at the table, enjoying the delicious treat while Carly beamed at the compliments floating through the air.

"Tell me again exactly what a housekeeper would do here," Janie said suddenly, putting her spoon down.

Neva sat back in her chair.

"Well, let's see. After the guests check out, the housekeeper is in charge of turning the room around to be readied for the next guests. Cleaning the bathrooms. Vacuuming or sweeping the floors. Taking trash out each day. Laundry—which is usually just towels and bedding but sometimes could include a change of clothes from a picky guest. Oh, ironing the sheets."

Janie cringed.

"But I could do the ironing," Neva added. "I don't mind it."

Just a little white lie.

"Or you could send them out," Carly said. "My best friend's mom sends all their bedding out to be done."

Neva didn't know about that, she'd have to find out the cost, but she nodded anyway. Now that she had them in front of her, she really wanted Janie to take the job. Having the girls around would be fun; she could just feel it.

"What about cooking?" Janie asked.

"I do the meals," Neva said. "I also take care of all the bookings and checking guests in and out. I set up tours for them if needed, or at least connect them to the appropriate party. I oversee all maintenance on the house and keep the accounts to make sure the taxes are paid. I have a gardener who keeps the property kept up, except for our family garden and I do that myself. Though for some reason, it has refused to bloom for the last few years and is looking a bit sad."

"Wow—that all sounds exhausting. I can't believe you take care of everything yourself," Janie said.

"Well, technically, I have help. When they show up."

"I could help cook," Carly offered, her expression hopeful.

"Well, that's mighty kind of you," Neva beamed. "But I'm sure you have studies to tend to."

Janie stood up and walked her bowl to the sink, setting it down gently inside. Then she turned back to Neva. "I'm sorry, I feel terrible, but I just can't see myself doing the job. As you could probably tell at our house, I'm not the best at keeping things orderly."

Breeze looked crestfallen. Carly had the manners not to appear happy, though Neva knew she probably was. "Well, that's fine. I'm still glad you came for dinner, and I appreciate you considering it," Neva said, trying hard to keep the disappointment from her voice.

Suddenly Charm made an appearance.

"Oh, what a pretty cat," said Breeze.

"That's Charm," Neva said and watched as the cat seemed to float across the kitchen floor and began weaving in and out of Janie's legs.

"She is pretty," Janie agreed. "I used to have a cat like her when I was a girl. I swear, she looked exactly like this one."

"She comes with the house," Neva said jokingly. "Ever heard of a therapy cat? Charm is our resident therapist and the sweetheart of Myster, who is hiding around here somewhere probably watching us. He got scolded this morning when I found him taking a nap on my rising bread dough. I guess he thought the towel over it was a blanket laid out just for him. He had a right cozy nap, he did."

Janie bent down to pet Charm and the cat purred up at her, her blues eyes locking on Janie's.

"Did I already say I'll take the job?" Janie looked up and said, a puzzled frown plastered across her face.

The girls looked confused, but Neva clapped her hands together and restrained herself from crouching down to throw her arms around Charm. She would be getting a can of premium tuna before bed, for sure.

"Oh, that's just wonderful. I'm thrilled, Janie."

"On one condition," Janie said, her face all smiles for the first time that Neva had seen, and what a gorgeous set of pearly whites she'd been hiding!

Charm had done a real number on her.

Neva waited.

Janie stood. "You have to let us move into the carriage house temporarily. I don't care what it looks like or how small it is. It can't be worse than where we are. We all hate that house and we're sleeping together anyway. It doesn't have a good energy about it. And I'm sure you can't afford to pay me what I'd need to stay in that dump *and* be able to put enough back for other expenses. I don't plan on living in Linden Falls forever and I need to save some money for where we are going next."

Neva didn't know what to say. The carriage house was not in any shape for anyone to dwell in, especially two young girls. Janie wouldn't be asking if she had seen it.

Not to mention it was really close to the house.

The fact that Loretta lived across town was usually a nice thing, as they needed that space after working together all day. However, Janie was probably correct. Neva couldn't pay a huge salary and probably not enough for what a mother needed to support two growing daughters.

She hesitated. If their room and board was free, then the salary she could offer just might be enough. She took a deep breath. "Yes, though you won't thank me once you've seen inside of it. But let's agree to a six-month trial partnership and then reevaluate. My housekeeper will probably be back by then and I can't pay you both, and you may find something more lucrative and want to move on anyway."

Janie nodded. "That could be, and it is a bit humbling that I have a master's degree in interior design and a minor in business, yet I'm going to be working as a housekeeper. When choosing my vocation, I neglected to notice that if you don't design, you don't get paid, and I sure can't do it from Linden Falls. So, we do what we have to do, right?"

Neva nodded. "We do. And humility is a wonderful lesson in selflessness. Some of the finest people I've known in my life work in service and hospitality. I appreciate you stepping up to get me out of a bind, and I hope your time here in Linden Falls will help you get to where you are needing to be yourself."

She didn't add that whatever it was that Janie was running from or to, hopefully the inn could be a respite along the way.

"Also, I'm going to put in a call that the Johnsons owe you a month of rent free for the shape that house is in. You can take that month to clean up the carriage house and get it livable."

"That would be great. Thank you," Janie said. "And by the time we are ready to go, hopefully I'll have it where you can rent it out if you like. But no promises, since I haven't seen it yet."

"I know the bones are good," Neva said. "It's just cluttered and dirty."

"Can I help fix it up, Mom?" Breeze said. "Pleeeease…"

"Of course. It's going to take all of us, judging by the look on Ms. Cabot's face when I asked," Janie said.

They all laughed. Neva a bit nervously because only she knew that it had been at least a decade since anyone had even ventured into the tiny cottage and she could just imagine the truly horrible state it was in. "And on that note, I really need to get this kitchen cleaned up so I can get to bed and be ready for guests in the morning."

Before she could even ask, both girls jumped to their feet and started clearing the table. Even Janie pitched in, and Neva had to admit, it almost felt like a family affair. One that made her hide her contented smile under an expression of tenacity to get the kitchen shining again.

CHAPTER 6

Two weeks to the day that Neva and Janie made their deal in the kitchen, she felt ashamed of herself as she hurried down the sidewalk. She cradled a stack of warm dishes and a squeeze bottle of dish detergent she'd felt led to grab from her sink on her way out. It was a beautiful Tuesday morning, but she felt bad because she'd let so much time pass after her offer to help with Greta.

It had been a busy time, hosting guests in and out while acclimating Janie to the routine at the inn until she and the girls all knew who was doing what and fell into their places.

They were a godsend, to be honest.

She saw the Harmon house and noticed it looked awfully still. A few rolled-up newspapers lay piled in front of the door.

Neva hoped Henry and Greta weren't away, but she

picked up her step. Her day was going to be a busy one, and she needed to utilize every minute to the fullest.

Thank goodness she had Janie keeping things up at the inn. For not thinking she had it in her to be a neat and tidy person, she'd easily picked up all the chores and, better than that, had written up a schedule of exactly what order they should be done in and how much time each took. She said it would help her—and later, Loretta—do more in less time.

Janie already accomplished more in one morning than Loretta did in a whole day, though Neva felt guilty for even thinking that about her old friend.

Loretta's temporary replacement was obviously very conscientious to give the amount of work she felt was deserved for her room, board, and small salary. Her pride was strong, and it was obvious that she wanted to feel like she was earning her way fairly before she disappeared out to the carriage house every afternoon for cleaning and organizing.

The girls did their classes online and had them done by midmorning, when they joined Neva and Janie at the inn. Their mom had done a wonderful job raising her daughters, because they were not afraid of work, and in addition to helping with the inn, Neva had seen them several times helping to bring a few pieces of old furniture and decorations down from the attic to be cleaned up and put in the carriage house.

One afternoon, Neva saw a tiny plume of white smoke coming from the front window of the little building. By the time she'd hurried out there, concerned, Janie had met her at the door and reassured her that nothing was wrong. She was simply cleansing any bad energy from the carriage house by burning sage.

"We have to ask the universe to release anything from inside that doesn't serve us in our highest power and reward," she'd said as she waved her hand over the small bowl of ash.

Neva was curious, but they wouldn't let her see inside until they were ready to move in. A surprise, Janie said, for her kindness. A grand reveal, Breeze called it in her excited and over-the-top style.

They didn't understand that they were giving far more than they were getting. Carly wouldn't even take any pay for her work. She'd insisted that she wanted to help prepare lunches for the guests, but she'd pretty much taken over and had already netted the inn several five-star reviews online because of her unique creations that made her guests feel like they were getting the total Vermont experience. So far, her best meal was the local venison, corn fritters, fiddleheads, and roasted butternut squash with maple syrup.

Neva was getting rounder as the days went by, but it might also be because she couldn't find the willpower to say no to Carly's desserts, either. The root beer float pie was to die for right along with the Indian pudding. Neva now went to bed at times with it on her mind. Oh, that thick porridge topped with molasses and cinnamon, a touch of ginger—it was just heavenly.

It amazed her how talented Carly was and so

willing to learn, too. She wasn't from Vermont, but with the internet to guide her and the freedom to experiment for finesse, no one would ever be the wiser. Neva already knew that she was going to make a wonderful chef one day.

At the bottom step of the house, she hesitated. It was only the second time she'd ever been to Henry's home, and it still felt a bit surreal that she was about to walk in as though nothing had ever happened between her and Greta.

But her grandmother had always reminded her that even if she lost everything, she would always hold three powerful resources that could never be taken away.

Love, prayer, and forgiveness.

The latter was the one she continued to remind herself of as she climbed the steps and rang the doorbell.

No one came.

A plaque next to the door was gathering dust.

Welcome to the Harmon House, it read. Inscribed along the bottom was Henry and Greta's names with the date their marriage was established. A date engraved in her own memory that she would never forget.

Let bygones be bygones, she told herself, then rang the bell again, just to be sure. She went to the porch swing and settled all the dishes there. Just when she turned to leave, the door opened, and Henry peeked out.

He looked terrible. Dark circles around his eyes. At least a week's growth of gray stubble on his face.

"Henry," she said, nearly stumbling over her words at the sight of him looking so haggard. He was usually meticulous about his appearance. "I brought you and Greta dinner for tonight."

He looked at the swing. "Thank you. I'll return your dishes, well...sometime."

"No hurry at all," Neva said.

He looked ready to shut the door.

"Just leave it there and I'll get it shortly."

"Wait, can I see Greta? Maybe give you some assistance this morning?"

"She's resting." He turned around and tilted his head inward to the house, as though listening for any indication that she was awake.

"Well, at least let me help you carry these in," Neva said, going to the swing for the dishes.

He sighed and joined her, picking up the casserole dish.

"I don't think you're going to give up, are you?"

Neva laughed softly, then followed him inside and to the kitchen.

It was a disaster.

"I know, I know," Henry said. "It's a mess. I ran out of dish soap, and we don't have a dishwasher."

She turned and looked at him after she set down her dishes and plunked the bottle of soap next to the sink.

"How did you know I needed that?" he asked.

"Never mind that. You look beat, Henry. I'm only going to say this once and I don't want to hear a bit of fussing. Go to your chair or your bed or wherever you like to relax, and lie back and close your eyes while Greta is quiet. I am not leaving until this kitchen is back in shape."

He stared down at her and they locked eyes in a battle of wills.

"It's bad, Neva."

"Tell me."

He raised his face and she saw the pain in it.

"Greta has gone downhill fast. She's arguing with me every minute and throwing tantrums when she doesn't get her way. Some days she even looks at me like I'm a total stranger. Then she had an ultrasound last week and it showed a large tumor on her right adrenal gland. More testing indicated it has spread to her lungs," he said.

"Cancer?"

"Yes. An extremely rare one. Aggressive, too. Adrenocortical carcinoma. It's not enough that she's slowly losing her memory. Now she's losing her life, too."

"What is the treatment plan? Chemo?"

He shook his head slowly. "The doctor recommended no treatment because the cancer is so far advanced in her system. He caught her at a moment of complete lucidity, and she agreed. She said she doesn't want to die looking like a shriveled-up, bald mushroom."

"So, she's choosing quality over quantity of life."

"I guess. Though with what she's going through losing a bit of herself every day with this damn dementia, I don't know what sort of quality we can call it."

"I'm so sorry, Henry," Neva said. And she was. No one deserved the double whammy that Greta was getting during her twilight years. "I don't know what to say during moments like this, so can you please just let me help in the only way I know how?"

He stared down at her.

"That means get out of this kitchen. Now."

He turned around and, shuffling slowly, disappeared out of the kitchen.

Neva felt a huge weight on her chest as she searched the drawers for an apron, then tied it on and rolled up her sleeves. She had always attacked her own home with a vengeance when she was feeling stressed out, and with the news about Greta, she felt a rush of energy.

With an expert hand and an occupied mind, she washed all the dishes, then the few pots and pans, grimacing when she saw the remnants of burnt eggs in one and some unknown crusty stuff in another.

One of them wasn't doing too well in the cooking department. But who could blame them when their world was falling apart around them?

In the overflowing trash can that peeked out from the pantry, Neva saw at least a half-dozen empty

Campbells soup cans and another pang of guilt hit her. She should've been bringing food over earlier.

After everything was washed, she found a bottle of spray cleaner and wiped down all the countertops. When she peeked into the refrigerator, she was horrified, and she moved in quickly to tackle it and avoid the Department of Sanitation from swooping in and declaring the house uninhabitable.

She knew she might be thinking a little dramatically, but a dirty refrigerator was something she couldn't stomach.

After unloading all the past-expiration condiments and scraping leftovers into the trash bin, she ran yet another sink of bubbles and knocked out those dishes, too. For some, it might take hours for such a complete job, but Neva had many years of practice and finished in just under an hour and just in time to untie her apron and turn to find Greta standing in the doorway, her mouth agape.

"So, it really is you," she said incredulously. "I thought when you turned around, my thoughts would be corrected, and you'd be someone Henry hired to come in and clean up his mess."

Neva pulled the apron from around her and folded it neatly, then laid it on the counter.

"It's me. In the flesh," she said. "And a lot of it."

Greta didn't smile at her attempt at humor.

"Why are you in my house? Already swooping in to try to claim Henry after I'm gone? What...you afraid one of the Winey Widows will grab him up before you can put your claim down?"

Neva nearly laughed at the thought of one of the women of the book club that met at Town Square Books wanting to get their claws into Henry, or him even being interested in them, but she saw how truly upset Greta was and held back.

"Now you should know that I'm happy to be the oldest town spinster and have no intention of ever giving up my title. I'm just here to help, Greta. I know you aren't feeling well, and I think Henry might be a bit exhausted."

Greta crossed her arms and leaned against the doorframe.

"So now I can't take care of my man?"

Neva did laugh that time. *Her man?* What were they doing? Starring in a sitcom? What eighty-year-old woman called her husband *her man*?

"Don't be ridiculous," Neva said, then steeled herself again. "If you want me to leave, just say so. But don't keep accusing me of preposterous notions."

Neva felt a rush of sadness that Greta was going to refuse her olive branch to put the past behind them. Had she forgotten their last visit when things went well? She always was a stubborn fool, but this was going to take the cake.

Suddenly Henry appeared behind her, running his fingers through his hair and blinking the sleep from his eyes.

"What's going on?" he said, stumbling into the kitchen.

Greta glared at him.

"Why don't you tell me, Henry Joseph Harmon? Why is *she* in our kitchen?"

Henry looked from Greta to Neva, then back again.

"I—I—" he stammered. "Now don't be getting all riled up before you let me explain."

Greta threw her head back and laughed uproariously.

"What's so funny, Greta?" Neva asked, her hands now on her own hips.

"I got you both," Greta said between guffaws.

Henry shook his head and went back to the living room, though Neva would swear he was shaking in his shoes for fear that he'd made Greta angry.

"That was uncalled for," Neva said to her.

She shrugged. "It's probably what he expected to begin with. I mean, after all this time, who would expect me to greet you graciously in my own home? Especially knowing that I'll be dead soon and the town widows really will be picking over everything I leave behind."

"Come sit down and let's talk," Neva said. "I'll make us some coffee."

"Only if you add a dash of whiskey to mine." Greta winked. "And only because for once in my life, I need a real friend and not just someone who sits at my table or wants something from me."

Neva nodded, though God knows she wasn't about

to give Greta any spirits to add to her sassy self. "Amen to that. Now sit your bossy tail down in the seat and tell me everything on your mind."

"You caught me on a good day," Greta said, taking a seat. "Yesterday my mind was on vacation. But we'd better talk fast before it decides to vacate again."

CHAPTER 7

*T*hey'd gone through a pot of coffee and were working on a second when Neva talked Greta into moving their talk out to the front porch. It was a beautiful day, and though they were getting closer to discussing the hard stuff, she wanted Greta to get as much fresh air as possible.

"You've had enough coffee," Neva said. "You'll never sleep tonight."

"Don't tell Henry how much I've had. He drugs me at night, you know. Always wants me sleeping so I won't bother him."

Neva recognized her statement for what it was, and it made her sad—suspicion and paranoia went hand in hand with dementia patients. Her own mother used to be afraid to eat for fear someone was poisoning her in the later stages of her own battle.

Henry had decided to walk into town for some grocery items, though Neva knew it was more about giving her and Greta privacy than anything else, but she was also glad that he was getting some time to himself. She could just see him now, sitting on the bench in front of the Wishing Tree, as she supposed that's where he went. He would probably be surprised that, so far, she hadn't had a bit of trouble with Greta.

Perhaps a change of who she was talking to was what she'd needed.

She held the hanging swing still so that Greta could get comfortable, then she sat down beside her. She avoided looking at her watch, but she knew she'd been gone too long from the inn and Janie might be getting worried.

Who knew when Greta might close the door on their friendship again? Neva was going to take every minute she could get, and hopefully at the end of it, Greta would agree to let her help Henry more often.

"Okay, where were we?" Neva said, settling her sweater closer around her middle to hide the extra pounds that showed up when she sat. She'd always been intimidated by Greta's good looks, and even now, when she was sick and it appeared that she had lost the obsession of full makeup from dawn until dusk, she still held a certain beauty that most women were jealous of.

"Tell me more about the girls," Greta said.

"Oh, yes. Breeze. She's the younger one and is who led me to them after she put a tiny fairy door at the Wishing Tree. She also hung a wish about her mom needing a job."

They had already talked about Janie, with Greta urging Neva to do an internet search and make sure she wasn't a criminal on the run. Her advice had made Neva chuckle.

Janie might be on the run, but Neva suspected it was either from a broken heart or a trail of bad luck, and nothing nefarious about it. She wouldn't meddle in her past because she wanted Janie to trust her enough to finally spill her story on her own, even if Neva felt deep down that there might just be a small mystery involved.

It would sort itself out. Or it wouldn't.

"I'm not surprised that you were sucked in by a fairy door," Greta said. "You were always infatuated with stuff like that when we were little."

Neva nodded. "You remember right. I was."

Greta leaned in. "I remember right, but you know who doesn't? Henry. On our ten-year anniversary he gifted me with a dollhouse that he said he spent a year secretly building. A little girl's dream with all kinds of fancy furniture and things with it. I believe he thought it was me that liked the miniature things."

"But I'm sure you loved it anyway," Neva said, thinking how absolutely thoughtful it was of Henry to create such a wonderful gift.

Greta shook her head. "You know me. I'm not into things like dollhouses, fairies, or wishing things. I'm practical. Give me diamonds. Or a Chanel purse. Or I would've rather he'd planned a trip to Italy. Or even Spain."

WISH YOU WERE HERE

"But you've been to both of those places."

That used to be a sore point for Neva, how Henry and Greta were always jet-setting around to different parts of the world, seeing new places and new faces, while Neva had never even left the county. She'd never had the funds to travel, though now that she was older and wiser, truth be told, she really didn't want to go through all the rigamarole it took to leave home. It was her safe place, and she did plenty of exploring the world through reading.

Secretly, though, the only place she held the smallest of dreams to see was Italy. Greta knew that once but had long ago forgotten it and probably had not given it a second thought when she'd landed there herself, instead of Neva.

Greta smiled. "Never enough traveling for me. That's one of my only regrets now. I won't be able to travel again. There are still a few places in the world that I wanted to see. But Henry says I'm too sick and we need to stay close to my doctors."

"Do you want to talk about that?"

A shadow of sadness crossed Greta's face.

"You know, I'm really not shocked about the cancer. I'm old and cancer isn't that uncommon to get as we age. But I do mind the problem with my memory. I'm forgetting huge parts of my life and sometimes I get so confused. It's truly terrifying and it's not fair. I've always taken great care of my mind."

Neva nodded. "I know you have."

Greta looked up at the sky. "I've been an avid

reader. I've kept my own accounts and even our joint accounts. Numbers, words...all that. Heck, I've even done a ton of puzzles in my time. Why is this happening to me?"

"I don't think it works like that, Greta. They don't really know why it happens to some and not others. I've done some reading in the last few weeks, and scientists are all in agreement that it's a combination of genetics, lifestyle, and environmental factors."

"Lifestyle? So, what are you saying? I drank too much? It was only a little wine here and there. It's not like I've buried myself in the bottle," Greta said, her tone defensive.

"No, that's not what I'm saying. I don't know. I don't think anyone really knows, and I agree, it's not fair. There are a lot of bad people in this world who get to live healthy lives. Why can't the illnesses find them and leave the good ones alone?"

"Oh, I've done bad things," Greta whispered.

"For goodness' sake," Neva said. "I'm sure you haven't committed anything too atrocious."

They swung back and forth in silence for a few minutes.

Greta was the first to speak again.

"You know, Neva, whenever I thought about the end, I always pictured myself surrounded by family and friends. But there really is no one left but Henry."

"You have me," Neva said.

"Well, that's a darn crazy miracle. But I should've had children. Henry wanted them so very badly."

"You can't redo the past, Greta."

"If I would've had children, then I'd have grandkids now, too. Maybe lots of them to gather round me and love me out of this world."

"At least you have a good husband. Be thankful for that," Neva said. "And let's not talk so morosely. I'm sure you have plenty of time left."

Greta raised her eyebrows at Neva.

"Okay, Miss Positive Pants. I'll play your game. If I had plenty of time and the health to do it, I'd travel. Henry and I would eat at all our favorite restaurants we've found. We would dance once again in the moonlight, swaying to the crooning of Tony Bennett or Bobby Darin."

Neva started to feel sick at her stomach.

"Greta, we're going to have to pick this up another time. I really need to get back to the inn."

"Oh…okay," Greta said.

"Before I go, I want to ask if you'd allow me to come visit you each morning for a few hours? Maybe help you with things."

"What kind of things?"

"Hmm…well, things like your hair. Or just whatever you might need. Things that a man can't do or do well. I have some tips and tricks that can help you navigate this frightening disease."

Greta looked away for a moment, as though in deep thought.

"I have a nurse that comes but she's sort of a biddy to deal with. So yes, I think I'd like that."

77

"Good deal. Now I'll be on my way, but I've left dinner for you both. Tell Henry to heat the casserole in the oven for half an hour with the tin foil on top."

She helped Greta from the swing, taking note of how drained she looked.

"I think I'm capable of heating up a casserole, Neva. Don't treat me like an invalid."

Neva laughed on her way down the porch steps. She was glad that Greta still had her sassy side. She was going to need all the gumption she could gather for what was ahead.

"Tomorrow," she said, waving behind her. She didn't look back to see what Greta did, for she feared that she might change her mind or forget what they were agreeing to.

On the other hand, as Neva headed toward home, she wondered if she was doing the right thing, because if she knew one thing at all, anything that had ever had to do with Henry and Greta was sure to break her heart.

CHAPTER 8

*N*eva looked up from her place at the kitchen table only to see Charm racing by, then a glimpse of pink with a leash trailing behind on the floor, backed up by Breeze hotfooting it through the kitchen in hot pursuit, straight out the back door. With only half an hour before Neva needed to meet a team at the Harmons' house, she didn't have time to ask where the pig's owner was and how Breeze had gotten stuck babysitting the quick little piglet.

Knowing Breeze, she'd probably begged to do it.

"Ms. Cabot, have you seen Myster today?" Janie said. She was coming through with a basket of soiled sheets and she paused.

"No, I haven't seen him since last night now that you mention it. He might be hiding from our new pink houseguest."

"Speaking of that, why in the world did the owner

name his pig Jimmy Dean? Doesn't that seem a little warped?"

Her rhetorical question made Neva chuckle. She held the pen to her lips, pausing as she stared at her last list of the day.

"Who knows why anyone does what they do these days? More importantly, where's the guest and why is Breeze on pig-sitting duty?"

Janie stopped and put the basket on the floor, then took a chair.

"He asked me first and I gave permission for her to spend her Saturday keeping Jimmy Dean on his hourly schedule of soccer practice while he takes a hike up to the falls," Janie said, not cracking a smile.

"Should I even ask about the soccer? I mean, is there a pig soccer league that I'm unaware of? Some new fad for the millennials to keep them occupied?"

"No. Nothing like that. He said that if Jimmy Dean doesn't get to push his soccer ball around outside every hour, he'll throw a fit and oink all night. Though with the setup he had in there for bedtime, I can't imagine the pig doing anything but lying back with his little paws crossed behind his head and sighing in ecstasy."

"Don't tell me he's in a playpen," Neva said. She was imagining the piglet with a watch wrapped around his hoof and a timer than went off every hour on the hour, reminding him to squeal for his soccer time.

"Better. He has a tiny wooden bed with his name engraved on the headboard. Complete with a mono-grammed coverlet and a pillow. His middle initial is *E*, by the way. I can only come up with Edward. Jimmy Edward Dean sounds about right."

Neva laughed. "Custom bed and monogrammed bedding for pigs isn't too over-the-top. I've had worse. You wouldn't believe what some people try to pass off as their emotional support animals. One man wanted to bring his llama in here. I was able to wiggle out of that one, and next to that request, I didn't bat an eye about Jimmy Dean."

Janie shook her head, a small smile across her face. "People are weird."

"A pig companion doesn't even make the list for weird here," Neva said. "I had one guest ask that his bed be made backwards, pillows at the end and his feet against the headboard. Another requested a room that the moon peeks in so she could sit in the moonlight for an hour before she slept each night. Oh, and how could I forget the guest who wanted a chocolate fountain to be waiting in her room upon her check-in, and for us to keep it going throughout her six-day stay."

"Did you do it?" Janie asked.

Neva shook her head. "No. I told her this wasn't the Waldorf. But I did leave her a box of specialty chocolates in the extensive pillow fort she also asked for. And no, there were no children with her. She was on a self-care retreat away from her family. I see some strange requests, but my mantra is that if it isn't costly and doesn't harm our house—and doesn't involve anything unsavory—I'll try to accommodate whatever floats their boat."

"You should write a book," Janie said, her smile bigger now. "All the happenings over the years here at the inn."

Neva raised her eyebrows, more at the smile than her words. Janie didn't let those happen often. Neva still wasn't sure what had brought them to Linden Falls or what they'd left behind, but Janie wasn't talking, and Neva wasn't prying.

"Now that's an idea. I mean, if I had time." She didn't mention the shelves of binder books that held decades of wishes and how much time it took to be the keeper of them. So far, she hadn't shared that with Janie or the girls. "But speaking of time, do you think you can handle things here until this afternoon? I'm meeting some workers over at my old friend's house. We don't have new guests coming until four o'clock and I'll be back by then."

Janie nodded. "Of course. Carly will be coming in a few minutes to start preparing for tonight, so we'll both be here. But I do want to ask you if you have anyone I can call to do some heavier work back in the carriage house for this afternoon?"

"What kind of work?" Neva said, hoping to get some information from her. They sure were keeping their project secret out there, and it was killing her not to know more.

"Just some stuff," Janie said. "It doesn't have to be anyone with a specialty. Just a strong set of arms will do."

Neva thought for a moment.

"Oh, I have the perfect person. A young man I know who is going to the prom probably needs to earn some more pocket change, especially considering his date is from the upper class of Linden Falls and who knows what she'll require on their special night. More than likely a limousine and the whole works."

Janie cringed.

"Did I say something wrong?" Neva asked, suddenly concerned.

"No, not your fault. It's just that Carly is missing her prom back home and she won't mention it, but I know it's a sore spot. But that will be fine. I'm sure he won't be talking about it. Just leave his number, please. I need to get this last load of sheets in so I can start ironing."

"He's a good boy. And I need to run, too." Neva jotted down the number for Jonathon and then gathered her notes and stood. A sharp pain made her pause, her hand on the table for support.

"Are you okay?" Janie said.

"I'm fine. Just stayed up too late getting ready for today. Now I need to gather everything up and get on over there."

"Can I help?"

"No, dear girl. You go ahead and wrestle the laundry. That's more help than I can even describe. Everything I'm doing is easy compared to your job. And by the way, we've never been so organized as we are with you here at the inn."

With that she hurried out of the kitchen. She'd already packed her little grocery cart, and she added the notes to the bag on top, then guided it all out the door.

She was on her way down the steps of the porch when she thought of one more thing. It wasn't something she thought Greta needed at this time, but now that it was in her mind, she would have to go up into the attic and find it, lest the thought pester her all day long.

Just as she lowered the cart to ground level, Breeze sped around the corner of the house, the piglet in her arms. Neva got a good look this time and thought the harness design of a barnyard full of chickens was quite ironic.

"Oh, Breeze, can you do me a favor?" Neva said. Her legs were already tired, and she had a short walk in front of her.

Neva told her what she needed and exactly where she thought it was sitting in the attic, then Breeze passed her the pig and ran inside.

"Oh. Well, hello, Jimmy Dean," Neva said, realizing she'd never held a pig before and wasn't sure if she could be trusted with the wiggling little fellow. "Why don't we sit right here and rest until Breeze comes back?"

She put him on the ground and lowered herself to the bottom step, the leash wound tightly around her hand. The pig didn't want to take off again, thankfully, and came closer, looking at her curiously.

"Go ahead. Look all you want. I know, I'm not as

young and shiny as your new sitter. This is what years of dealing with guests like you will do to a face."

She could swear by the way Jimmy Dean watched her talk that he understood everything she was saying. She prayed he wouldn't slip into a squealing fit, so she kept talking, telling him he'd better not have any concessions of courting Charm because Myster would put him in his place, but maybe they could ask around town and see if there was a pretty pink piglet girl for him to have a playdate with.

He must've liked that idea, because he came close to her feet and curled his lips, then huffed a puff of hot air on her. Then he plopped over, landing on his side, belly pointed her way.

Neva gingerly reached out and gave him the belly rub he was so shamelessly asking for, and she smiled as he closed his eyes in rapture and let his tiny pink tongue hang out.

Breeze came out the door, clumsily holding the last-minute item that was taller than she was. She saw the piglet lying splayed out on the walkway.

"Oh, that means he likes you, Ms. Cabot," she said. "Did he blow on you? They huff on you if they trust you, Mr. Hinson said."

Neva got to her feet and brushed the piggy germs off her hands.

"He sure did. I feel very honored, too. And thank you so much for running up those stairs for me, Breeze, but I need to hurry on."

She took the item from the girl, and with one hand

holding it and the other pushing her cart, she left Breeze and the piglet at the bottom of the steps and took off down the sidewalk. She wasn't sure what would greet her at the Harmon house or if they were going to welcome her ideas, but there was no better time than the present to find out.

CHAPTER 9

*H*enry put his head in his hands, unable to watch his wife any longer. For the last hour, she had been having a very heated conversation at the table, her hands moving frantically as she talked, most of her words mumbled incoherently and aimed at an invisible guest in their kitchen.

She'd refused to eat and that meant he hadn't yet given her any medication, but he needed a moment before trying to tempt her again. She hadn't even allowed him to help her out of her nightclothes, and she'd skipped her morning hygiene routines again.

As she talked, he caught a word or two here and there. It seemed she was planning an event. Menus, lighting, and flowers were a few things he'd heard in her rant.

After a morning of her following him around so close he swore he could feel her breath on his neck, he was relieved to have a minute of peace to himself. He wasn't mad at her. He knew she wasn't herself. But only because she was running on fumes, and in her exhausted state, her mind was taking advantage to torment her further. Or at least that was his humble opinion of her sudden decline into talking to someone who wasn't there.

He was exhausted, too. They'd been up since three that morning after Greta had catapulted herself out of her bed and landed on the humidifier he'd plugged in just beside her on the floor.

It wasn't clear why she'd taken the leap, but they were lucky it wasn't more serious than it was. And next time...well, he didn't even want to think of what could've happened.

Greta was bruised but swore there was nothing broken and refused to get dressed so he could take her to be looked over at the clinic.

Now he cursed himself for letting her sleep in her room alone, as well as allowing such a break in their routine the day before when Neva had visited. Since then, Greta had not been herself, slipping in and out of a few tantrums when she couldn't find the words to tell him why she was upset.

He wasn't looking forward to telling Neva he didn't want her to come back, but they should've known that they couldn't suddenly put decades of history behind them as water under the bridge, especially at such a delicate time as now, when Greta was just doing her best to survive.

It was too much. His wife needed things to be quiet

and to keep things as close to their normal routine as possible. That meant just the two of them, other than their no-nonsense nurse, who did only what was required and in a hurry at that, before she fled out the door and left them to handle the rest of the day and night alone.

Even that was starting to make him nervous, but Greta needed him to be her advocate, and that meant it was his duty to protect her from herself and from the things that would upset her current fragile existence.

A knock at the door startled them both, and Henry looked at his watch, dismayed to see it was already time for Neva to arrive. He'd wanted to have a bit more time to keep Greta still in the hopes to get her settled down enough to get some food in her before starting the negotiations for her medicine.

Now she was up and headed to the foyer.

He followed and was standing behind her when Greta opened the front door and saw Neva there. "What?" she said, her voice tinged with irritation.

"Good morning, Neva," Henry said, trying to soften Greta's greeting. There was no need to be rude.

"Well, hello to you both," Neva said, smiling as though she wasn't just welcomed with the most unwelcoming show ever.

"Go away," Greta said.

"Feeling crabby today? Let's see if I can help," Neva said, then dragging a cart behind her, she proceeded through the door with enough purpose that both he and Greta stepped aside to avoid being trampled on.

"I–I wanted to talk to you first," Henry sputtered. "Maybe outside?"

Greta shot him a look that could kill, and Neva shook her head.

"Nope. Bring in that contraption I leaned next to the door and we can talk in here. Whatever you want to say to me you can say in front of your wife."

Behind her Greta huffed but said nothing, probably because it appeared that Neva was on her side—as though there were sides and any type of battle lines. Henry did as he was told, knowing that once two stubborn women got together and joined forces, the best thing was to just shut up and do their bidding.

He grabbed the long piece of something that was on the porch and brought it in. "What is this?"

Neva parked her cart next in the hallway.

"It's a bed rail. You tuck the stabilizer under the mattress, and it'll keep Greta from falling out during the night. Maybe also keep any restless wandering down to a minimum."

Henry didn't know how Neva did it, but she was always delivering things that people needed before they even knew they needed them. Too bad her delivery wasn't one day earlier this time. They might've gotten more sleep. However, the challenge would be getting Greta to allow him to put the protector into place so that maybe they could avoid any more unfortunate accidents.

"First things first," Neva said. "Have we all had breakfast?"

"He hasn't fed me a thing," said Greta. "I'm starving."

Henry started to correct her, but Neva held her hand up, stopping him mid-sentence.

"Let's take care of that right now, then get down to business."

He watched as she defused the situation with just a few words and headed into the kitchen, Greta following.

Might as well join the circus instead of just watch. He trailed behind like a little duckling and settled himself at the table.

Neva chattered along about the town happenings as she deftly put together a huge omelet, then divided it into three pieces on three plates, garnished with buttered toast, and set it before them. She poured juice for them all and sank into an empty chair, said the blessing, then picked up her fork and began eating.

It was astounding how easily she managed it all and hadn't even broken a sweat. Henry knew he was a lot less graceful in the kitchen. More like a bull in a china shop.

"Might be a good time to take your medication, Greta," he said, offering some sort of contribution, then pushed the weekly pill container over to her side.

Greta picked it up and first opened the wrong day of the week. Neva quietly and gently closed that flap and pointed at the correct one, and Greta emptied the pills into her hand, then tossed them down with a swig of juice.

Henry thought about asking her why she was so

easy to work with when Neva was there but instead concentrated on eating his breakfast before things went awry again.

Suddenly he caught the corner of something black under the table and it startled him. He nearly knocked his chair over backwards, he moved so fast.

"What in tarnation is that?" he said, peeking under the table.

Neva and Greta both peeked beneath.

"Well, there you are, Myster. How in the world did you get in here?" Neva said, clucking her tongue at the cat.

"A cat," Henry exclaimed. "We don't have a cat."

"He must've come in with me," Neva said. "I didn't see him, but I'll claim the little minx. I'll just go put him outside. He can find his way home."

Greta waved her hand in the air.

"Oh, no, you don't. That's my friend. He lay in the bed with me this morning."

Henry stared at Greta, then looked at Neva. He didn't know what the heck was going on, but his wife had decided long ago after their one and only pet had died, that she never wanted animals in the house again.

"That's good, Greta. Myster can be a real comfort. I'm glad you found each other."

Henry sat back down and watched, speechless as Greta reached down and petted the cat that was now rubbing itself all over her legs. He felt a rush of sadness. The Greta he knew truly was slipping away.

Neva finished her food and took her plate to the

sink, squeezed detergent in, and then ran it full of hot, soapy water.

"Come on, Greta," she said. "Finish up and get over here and wash these dishes."

Greta had never liked cleanup duty, but she quietly picked up her plate and went to the sink, then started washing, rinsing, and setting the dishes in the rack.

Neva was making her way around the countertops with a damp paper towel. She came and picked up Henry's plate and fork and took them to Greta.

"We are going to put together a task list and schedule of what to do each day," Neva said, coming to stand near the table. "We'll print them up on sheets of paper and each night lay them out on your bench in the foyer, which we will now call the *memory bench*."

"Like what tasks?" Henry asked.

"Whatever should be done every day. Shower. Get dressed. Cook breakfast. Eat. Clean up."

"I think we know those things, Neva," Greta said.

Henry silently agreed.

Neva nodded. "Yes, you probably think you do. But there will be days that both you and Henry are too tired to think, and the lists will make things easier. Keep you on track, if you will. And I've already got a few papers done and ready. Later we'll work on lists for your bills to be paid."

She went to her cart and pulled out a folder, then took a stack of papers from it and laid them side by side on the bench.

Henry and Greta followed her, then stood over the papers, reading each one.

He was afraid what his wife's reaction would be to someone micromanaging her every hour, but surprisingly, he could see her nodding her head as she read. Then she looked up.

"I like this. Now will you help me do something with myself? I think I look a fright."

Neva and Henry laughed at Greta's honesty, and he watched as they left him and headed toward the bedroom.

"I'm pretty sure I have it down on your list for today to take the trash out and sweep off the front porch, Henry," Neva called out as they disappeared.

He shook his head.

Now he'd have two women telling him what to do. He predicted he was going to be a very busy man, and probably one who'd soon be ready to pull out his own hair.

Or what was left of it.

PART II

The
Wishing Tree
SERIES

CHAPTER 10

*N*eva inhaled and let the crisp scent fill her up as she closed her eyes to take a moment to enjoy it. The house had never smelled so good or sparkled as much as it did now. It was quiet, too, now that the last guests had gone, and they thankfully were going to have the inn to themselves until the weekend.

At first when Janie had told her about the herbal cleansing ritual and asked if Neva minded, she wasn't sure what she thought. She didn't like delving into witchy things and wondered if this was straddling the line of being too new age or weird. However, once Janie explained—and she didn't force the idea, either—it made sense. Still, it was strange that a woman who held a career in interior design was so interested in potions and such.

"Tell me again what was in it," Neva opened her eyes and asked.

Janie turned from her place at the sink.

"Nothing complicated. Just fill your bucket with pieces of fresh rosemary and pour boiled water over it. Add a few drops of lemon essential oil and a quartz crystal if you have one. I covered it with a cloth and let the herbs steep for half an hour, then took out the crystal and the herbs and it was ready to go."

"That's the best-smelling mop water I've encountered yet," Neva said. "I usually only mop with vinegar water and a bit of dish soap, other than every other week when Loretta uses Murphy's oil."

"This isn't about deep spring cleaning. It's to carry out the stagnant energy. Before you start using it, you are supposed to close your eyes and think about what you want to feel when you step into the room. Peace. Joy. Inspiration, if it's your office or work room. It's all about setting an intention. Most people do it at the end of winter, but after our last guests, I felt like we needed it now."

Neva chuckled. "Yes, I get some doozies here. I'm sorry I've been so wrapped up with the Harmons and it's all fallen on you. But I'm also very grateful you are here."

Breeze came into the kitchen.

"Oh, are you talking about the Crawfords? He was disgusting."

"Whoa, you little eavesdropper," Janie said. "But you're right on both counts."

"I can't believe he shaved that long beard completely off and just left all the hair on the floor," Neva said. "Some people have no manners whatsoever."

"He also came downstairs in his underwear this morning looking for coffee," Breeze said. "Carly told him to turn around and go back to his room and get dressed, that it wasn't appropriate for me to see. But I've seen Dad in his underwear plenty of times and it's not that big of a deal."

"Breeze!" Janie said, her voice steely. "Go outside. Now."

Neva felt an awkward silence fill the air as Breeze looked instantly chastised and skirted out the back door without another word.

It wasn't the first time lately that she'd mentioned her father, and it made Neva sad that she wasn't allowed to talk about him. From the little bit she'd gathered, they were separated but not because of anything too terrible.

"You know, I was thinking," Janie said. "The sunroom could be so gorgeous with a bit of updating, and you could open it up as a tearoom. Offer small plates. Scones, muffins—that kind of thing—but for the public and not just the inn guests. Bring in some additional income."

"Hmm...that does sound nice. But it would be a lot of work. I'd have to hire more help, I suppose. But I'll definitely put that on the list of ideas to consider. I do love making my scones and muffins. And I'm sure Carly could come up with some new recipes."

"She'd love that. And really, we wouldn't need to do much to get it going. You already serve tea and tidbits to your guests. Just open it to others, too." Janie turned back to the sink, where she was washing the last dishes from lunch. A really good one at that— a sausage and ricotta naan pizza Carly had whipped up.

It was a good idea. Come to think of it, Janie had a lot of great ideas, Neva thought. She took a long sip of her tea, a brown sugar cinnamon tea latte that Janie had turned her on to and now she couldn't do without to get her going. The girls were spoiling all the guests, as well as expanding Neva's waistline one scrumptious recipe at a time.

Carly allowed everyone to help her prep, but she insisted on cooking most of the meals, a blessing considering all the time that Neva was spending with Greta now.

Seven weeks had flown by since that first day when she'd dug in to try her best to make the horrible disease of Alzheimer's and her diagnosis of cancer a bit easier to live with.

For the most part, both Henry and Greta followed the task sheets laid out on the memory bench each night for the next day's events. But Greta's cognitive functions were declining at a faster pace than either Neva or Henry expected, and just the day before, they'd hung a new checklist in the shower, protected by plastic and bright with bulleted and simple reminders.

Take off your clothes.
Turn on shower.
Turn left for warm, then test water.
Step into shower stall.
Wash your hair.

Rinse your hair.

Wash your body.

Rinse. Dry off and get out.

These were things that most people did with muscle memory and not much thought, but Greta was struggling with figuring out what she once knew by heart. Along with that, her latest cancer scan showed rapid growth, and the pain and nausea that came with all that made Greta very uncomfortable and sometimes that meant unmanageable.

It was a lot.

But Neva wouldn't have it any other way. She could never leave Henry to handle it alone. And Janie was the reason she was able to juggle it all. She was so grateful to her.

"Janie, why don't you come have some tea with me?"

"I think I'll do just that," Janie said. "My back is hurting a bit today."

"Well, no wonder it is. With all you've done to get that carriage house looking like it does, I'm surprised you can still walk. Any of you."

The makeover that Janie had given the old house was nothing less than amazing. Many years ago, it had been made livable, but now it was a showpiece. It had started out as a barn back in the old days, and Janie had even made the old loft into a small bedroom for the girls.

She'd brought down several antique pieces of furniture from the attic and used them to accent the modest setting, making it warm and cozy, with shades of deep burgundy and forest-green coverings and curtains.

Janie had moved all the old boxes away from the back wall window and made it a focal point that looked out into the private Cabot garden, which had bloomed for the first time in years with pile upon pile of honeysuckle climbing the trellis and snaking across the fence in a joyous display of eagerness. A dogwood tree that was thought sure to be dead had also come alive, its branches full of green leaves as they reached for the sky and white berries hanging low and plump to be picked by the birds that sang out every morning.

It seemed the entire place was happy with the arrival of Janie and her girls.

As for the carriage house, Neva was blown away by the talent it took to bring it all together and make it a private space that, in the future, tenants would be clamoring to rent. Somehow Neva felt like she was getting the better end of the deal with the three of them, even Breeze, who always brought a shot of optimism with her everywhere she went.

Janie poured some water over a tea bag and brought the mug to the table. She sat across from Neva. "If it wasn't for that Jonathon, we'd be in worse shape. He's been a huge help and is so willing to work hard for a little bit of money."

Neva nodded. "He needs it, considering he's taking the Wilbanks girl to the prom. She'll expect the red-carpet treatment."

Janie laughed. "Yeah, we've heard a bit about her. He

offered to introduce her to Carly so she'd have a new friend, but she declined. She's happy just having Jonathon to come by and keep her company and regale her with his stories of working in the orchards. He's got a way with words."

Neva nodded. "Yes, he does. He's a talker, as they say. I see that Breeze is loving that tire swing he put up for her. That was nice of him."

Janie stared out the window of the door behind Neva.

"I suppose you don't approve of the way I scolded her," she said quietly.

"It's not my place to approve or not, though I'll admit it squeezes my heart a bit to see her sad. She seems to be mentioning her dad more these last few weeks."

"I've told her not to," Janie said. "It just makes everyone feel uncomfortable."

Neva raised her eyebrows, bit her lip, then decided that it needed to be said.

"Everyone? Or just you?"

Janie stiffened. "You don't know the whole story."

"You are right about that, and it's none of my business. I'm here if you need to talk, and if you don't, I'll respect that, too. He must not be a good man for you to have taken off and he's not even getting to see his girls. A mother does what she must."

Charm sauntered into the kitchen and under the table, then began rubbing herself along Janie's legs as she purred for attention. She was a bit offput lately, as

Myster still hadn't come home from the Harmon house, despite Neva's attempts to tempt him back.

"Oh, he's a good man," Janie said, her tone more than a little defensive.

Now Neva was confused.

Janie explained. "He doesn't know where we are. I needed some space and didn't want him breathing down my neck while I thought things over."

"Oh dear," Neva said. "Honey, does he know you and the girls are safe? I can't imagine how worried he might be."

"He knows. I drove over the state line and sent him a postcard last week."

They both sipped at their tea, lost in thought.

When Neva sneaked a peek, she saw a tear slide down Janie's nose and drop right into her mug with a silent splash.

She'd not yet witnessed that kind of emotion from her, and it made her want to jump out of her chair and rush to put her arms around the girl. But Janie wasn't that type, and a flood of love would surely send her bolting from the kitchen.

Neva had to let it play out.

She called it right, because finally, Janie started to talk.

"This sounds so cliché, but I think I'm having a crisis of identity. I never knew my own father, but I knew who he was and the general area he'd settled in. With the ease of social media now, I could've sought him out to try to have a relationship with him."

"That goes both ways," Neva said, her tone gentle. "Don't take all the blame. I see so many parents just leave their children in the dust as they start new lives, not understanding that those children become adults with huge holes in their hearts that stepparents may not ever fill, no matter how loving they are."

Janie nodded. "Mom never married. But honestly, my biological father never knew about me. It's not his fault."

"Oh. Well, that's hard." Neva didn't want to judge her mother, but she couldn't imagine why the woman would keep that sort of secret and keep a father from his child.

"My husband, Max, didn't know the details because I always pretended it didn't bother me not to have a father in my life. But when my mom found out he died and she told me, I felt such a huge loss, even though I never knew him. I fell into a bit of a depression and Max just wasn't getting it. He has both parents. He got to know what it was like to grow up with both mother and father to lead him, teach him, and just love him. I wanted him to understand my loss. Even though I was grieving someone who I never knew."

"Of course you were," Neva said. Unable to help herself, she reached over and patted Janie's hand. "Every woman has that little girl inside her who wants her daddy's love and approval. You never got it, and when he died, your heart knew it was too late to ever have it. That's understandable. I'm surprised your husband didn't realize it."

"I never tried to explain, I guess. I just felt that, after seventeen years together, Max should already know—without me saying the words of what was so wrong inside. And when he didn't, my anger turned toward him. I told him he doesn't really know me. We fought. I left."

She said it so matter-of-factly, but Neva could feel the pain in her words. Maybe even the regret.

"Now I've never been married, so I'm no expert, but I'm pretty sure that most men have to be hit over the head with a literal bat of intention before they *just know* what they need to know about their ladies. They aren't the most intuitive beings in the world."

Janie smiled and it encouraged Neva to probe a bit deeper.

"How do you feel now, since you've had some time apart? Do you miss him?" Neva asked.

She hesitated. "Yes. I do. And I feel guilty about the girls not seeing him, even though he's usually away on business and is rarely home. He only spends about one weekend a month with us, if that."

Another hint.

"Sounds to me like you may be feeling a little neglected by him, too. I suppose the combination of your father dying and your husband not being there for you sent you into a spiral. I'm so sorry. But Janie, you must let the girls see their father. You don't want to do to them what your mother did to you."

Janie looked torn. "I know. And I'm going to reach out to him soon. Every night before I go to sleep, I promise myself I'll do it in the morning. But I also feel like, for the first time in my life, I'm making a success of myself without someone else as a crutch. I mean, I know this isn't my place. But...I do feel attached to it."

Neva smiled. "This inn has a way of doing that to people for sure. But, well, this time it feels different with all of you here. Like—and this is going to sound strange—but like it's happy again. I've never seen honeysuckles grow like that out there. They were planted in honor of my great-grandmother, Honey. I feel like she's around here again, peeking in on our progress."

"See? That's what I mean. You have roots here. Stories that are attached to this house. Things I never got because my mother was also a loner and didn't have much to do with her people. I don't know anything much about any of my relatives. And that feels wrong and makes my soul feel empty."

Neva stood and followed her instinct.

She went around behind Janie's chair and leaned down, wrapping her arms around her and giving her a reassuring squeeze.

"But don't you see, dear girl? You can make your own roots. Your daughters are your legacy, and then their children, and on and on. Don't you know how lucky you are?" She stopped then, just short of blurting out her life's regret of not having a family to call her own.

This wasn't about her. It was about trying to make

Janie see that you can't change the past, but you can always make your future what you want it to be.

Her phone rang out and she glanced down at it.

Henry.

Normally he didn't call her because he knew she'd show up when she said, and no matter what she'd try to tell him, he'd refused to ask her to come any other time, even when Greta was having an episode. He said again and again that she was doing too much for them.

She picked up the phone and hurried into the sunroom.

"Hello? Henry?"

CHAPTER 11

*H*enry felt like the walls were closing in on him as he waited for Neva to answer the phone. When she did and he explained, he was relieved to hear her say she'd be right over. He hung up the phone and hurried back to Greta.

She still sat in the empty bathtub, dressed in flowered pajamas with her legs outstretched and her arms crossed over her chest. The nurse had left earlier, tired of attempting to get Greta to cooperate and taking advantage of the situation to skip out early.

"Please talk to me, honey," Henry said, taking his seat on the toilet again.

She hadn't said a word to him since the evening before when they'd taken a stroll. They'd landed at the town square and gravitated toward the Wishing Tree, to see if any new wishes were hanging, as they'd done often for many, many years.

Greta was having a good day. She'd wanted to go.

However, once there, she couldn't remember what a bench was called, and then she couldn't recall what she'd written on her one wish so many years ago. That had bothered her more than anything to date, because she knew it was important, and she'd thought about it for decades but now just could not remember what it was.

She'd gone to bed without any fuss. Without any words at all, actually. And ironically, this morning she hadn't forgotten about it. She was still upset.

"You need to take your pain medicine, Greta. But you have to eat first. Please—I'm asking you nicely. Neva left some pancakes yesterday. I can heat them up. How about that?"

She turned her head toward the tiled wall.

Henry hated the silent treatment more than any punishment that Greta had dished out over their marriage. It always brought his own memories of his childhood to the forefront, the tense dinners around their table when his father was in one of his moods, the way they all mechanically did their chores and hurried off to their rooms for the night.

He'd explained that to Greta more than once over the years and asked her not to use that mode of passive-aggressive emotional sparring with him, and for many years she'd respected his confession and request.

Her tongue-lashings were legendary after that.

Now, when he missed her the most and could find comfort that even if she wasn't totally *with him* much of the time, she was still physically there, having conversation, it seemed it was once again going to be her secret weapon.

She couldn't be held accountable for it, though. Henry knew this. But it didn't stop him from despairing.

He missed Greta.

His Greta. The spicy-tongued, high-energy, and driven woman she used to be. This was getting harder every day.

Myster sauntered in and, with a graceful leap, was over the side of the tub and landing in Greta's lap. He looked up at her, puzzled, and meowed.

"That's not your cat," Henry said, hoping to get her fired up.

She didn't respond and Myster circled twice, then curled up on her belly, his dark eyes locked on Greta's.

Henry heard her sigh, then she unlocked her arms from across her chest and put her hand on Myster and moved her fingers.

That was a start.

He heard a knock on the door and rushed up so fast from his seat that he felt light-headed and remembered he also hadn't had breakfast or even his coffee. He hurried to the door and flung it open.

"Good Lord, what did you do, helicopter over here?" he asked.

"Well, it's only a ten-minute walk on an easy day. I rushed. Where is she?" She carried a canvas tote bag with an old Norman Rockwell calendar sticking out of it and bustled past him.

"Still in her bathroom."

He followed Neva but stopped short of going into the bathroom with her. Greta usually behaved better with Neva when he wasn't present, so he sat down on the bed.

"Good morning, Greta," Henry heard Neva say.

No response.

She continued. "And to you as well, Myster. I know a lovely lady cat named Charm who is getting very impatient waiting for her sweetheart to come home."

"Well, it's okay if you don't want to talk to me," Neva said. "I know that it's hard to realize you are losing some of your memories. It's not fair. But you know what? I still remember how, when we were best friends, you used to inspire me with your storytelling abilities."

Silence. Then Henry heard her rustling with what sounded like paper.

Neva started again. "I picked this old calendar up at a yard sale a few months ago, though I had no idea what I'd do with it. I'll bet you a dollar that you can still just look at one of the pictures and come up with a story right off the top of your head. Take this one for starters. I see an old man impatient for the bus to show up and take his son off to the city for school. He wants to get back to work. What do you see?"

First there was nothing more but the incessant and constant ringing in Henry's ears.

"That's not his father."

Henry pumped the air with his fist. That was his Greta's voice, no doubt.

"Who is it, then?" Neva asked.

"His uncle."

"Where's his parents?"

"They died when their old truck blew a tire and ran off the road. It flipped. Johnny and the dog crawled out from the wreckage, and he didn't know the uncle, but it was his only family left."

"See, I told you!" Neva said. "Storytelling is such an ancient form of communication, and you are so good at it that, even though you might not be able to access some of your memories, this shows your brain is still working. It's not over yet, Greta. You're a fighter and you can't give in. So, get up and let's start this day."

Neva was a genius. Greta always did respond to accolades.

Then he heard Greta give a hmmpf.

"The dog is sad because the boy is leaving, and the uncle pretends not to like him. The dog, I mean. Or the boy, really. But deep inside he's really suffering to see them go. He spent his last five dollars to buy the boy a suit and good shoes, and his latest crop will pay the tuition. He never got along with his brother, and this is one way he can make amends."

Henry couldn't believe his ears. Greta hadn't sounded that clear or detailed about anything in nearly a year.

Neva let out a long laugh.

"I love it! You still got it. I've got some more pictures, too. But please, get your lazy butt up out of that tub and let's pick out something pretty to wear today. We'll show that hubby of yours that you're also still the looker he picked out to be his."

Henry cringed at those words, and he stood, then tiptoed out of the room and went to the kitchen. While he started a pot of coffee, he thought about Greta's details about the picture. It had to be an old print of Rockwell's famous *Breaking Ties* painting. Ironically, he knew it very well. A copy of it used to hang in the living room of his childhood home.

He puttered around, getting out the skillet. Then the bacon, eggs, and milk from the refrigerator. The pancake idea was history, as he wasn't about to suggest she have leftovers now that she was cooperating.

He peeled the slabs of bacon from the package and laid them in the skillet. Greta liked Neva's cooking better, but he could at least help prep while he waited for them.

While he was cracking the eggs into a bowl, she showed up.

"Where's Greta?"

"She wanted a minute to herself. She's fine," Neva said.

She had her canvas bag with her and pulled out two jars of brown liquid.

"What is that?" he asked.

"I'm not really sure but something that Janie whipped up with some of her herbs that she said will help Greta feel less nauseated. It's to be heated in the kettle and drunk like a tea before bed."

Henry didn't know what to say about that, so he went and washed his hands, then turned around. "I'm sorry I had to call you over early."

"Pshht," Neva waved a hand in the air. "Don't say another word. That's what friends are for."

"Friends usually do for each other," he said. "I've done nothing for you, and you are spending most of your time caring for my wife."

Neva took the bowl of eggs and poured a bit of milk in, then started mixing.

"Now you know I'd do it for anyone in Linden Falls. That's what I do, Henry. Always have, always will."

"But after—"

She held her hand up, stopping him.

"I've told you not to talk about the past and I mean it. We aren't there anymore. We are here. Greta needs us both."

Henry took a seat at the table.

"What was that in there? How did you know to get through to her like that?" he asked.

"It's a program I help Faith and Penny lead out at the senior center called Time Slips. It's a form of creative engagement that's therapeutic for people who have dementia. They don't get frustrated because they don't have to remember anything, just make things up as they go."

"That's brilliant. Greta used to love telling tall tales."

"I remember," Neva said, smiling over her shoulder.

"And this way she still feels that her brain is working. It can give her some hope that there's still more time."

Time. He knew it was running out.

"I wonder if there's some way you can look up her wish?" he said.

Neva turned and held up the whisk. "No. First, I don't remember ever plucking one off the tree that looked like her handwriting. And even if I did, it would take forever to go through all the binders to try to find it. I wouldn't do that unless she specifically asked me to, during a time I know she is completely in the moment. That would be an invasion of her privacy, Henry."

He nodded. "Fine. I didn't think of it that way. Let's don't bring it up because I don't want another evening of the silent treatment."

"Henry, you have to separate yourself from Greta's issues. You are doing just fine with her. Please, give yourself some credit for the strength you are showing. You can't rescue every situation."

"I don't know," Henry said. "It doesn't feel like enough."

Neva turned back around to her task, just as Greta came in.

"Well...wow—you look nice," Henry said.

Greta smiled, a bit seductively, if he was honest with himself.

He didn't tell her that her red lipstick wasn't perfect.

"I can still turn a few heads," Greta said, then took a

seat at the table next to him. "Even if mine is a bit, shall we say, *naughty* much of the time these days."

"Naughty is a word that fits you well, dear," Henry said, chuckling. "Thank you for getting dressed and for coming in for breakfast. Let me get your medication."

He got up from the table and went to the counter. He would do whatever it took to give his wife a good day and make up for her despair over the forgotten wish. He spoiled her. But Greta would always have a hold over him.

Despite all they'd been through, he only wanted to see her happy.

Or at least not on the warpath.

And Neva, well...he didn't know what to think about her. There were so many emotions tied up with their history that he just couldn't go there. Not when it was taking every bit of energy he had to just get through Greta's crisis.

CHAPTER 12

*N*eva took a long sip from her glass of lemonade and sighed contentedly at the sound of the girls scraping their feet against the porch floor with each pass of the swing. Janie sat in the chair beside her, lost in thought as she rocked back and forth. Even Charm accompanied them, a surprise considering how surly she was since Myster had stopped coming home.

Evenings spent on the front porch of the inn were once again a routine since they'd moved in. Once they had all chores completed and things prepped for the morning, and the girls finished any homework, they met there for at least an hour to wrap up the day.

Sometimes Carly didn't come out, depending on if she was having a good teenager day or was mad at the world. But Breeze looked forward to it as much as Neva.

They were a little late tonight, as they'd all worked

together to finish up the nifty coffee station that Janie started. Now her early-rising guests didn't have to wander into the kitchen in their underwear looking for a cup of joe. After Janie was through, the old antique cabinet in the upstairs hallway looked completely different with the cute shelf above it, the mugs hanging across the wall, and all sorts of unique touches that instantly attracted you to come near.

Janie had even added the sweetest glass bottles of raspberry, vanilla, and caramel syrups for specialty drinks. Each had scalloped vintage labels hanging from them for identification.

Neva wasn't sure why she'd never thought of the idea herself, as it was going to make her life so much easier. Guests in the kitchen were one of her pet peeves. Now they would have fresh muffins set out on her grandmother's antique cake stand, and even fruit for quick snacks there, too.

It was a day well done, as her mother used to say.

Neva loved porch time. Especially when she had someone to spend it with. Sometimes a friend or two stopped by and took a seat for a moment, exchanging town news. So far, the Linden Falls grapevine hadn't done much to reveal any details about who Neva had living in her carriage house, or not enough to satisfy some of the wagging tongues.

Neva always guarded Janie's privacy, even when the nosiest of neighbors tried to pry. Two of her oldest friends, Agnes and Cecilia, had nearly burst a blood vessel when they'd left the porch with nothing more than first names a week before. Neva didn't give in, and that just whet their curiosity more, knowing that she was so protective of them.

"Tell me more about what it was like growing up with your brother," Janie said. "I never had siblings."

Neva smiled. Greta wasn't the only storyteller in town, because Janie and the girls couldn't get enough of her tales about growing up in Linden Falls.

Most evenings she'd rather hear Carly and Breeze chatter on about this and that, reveling in their youth and excitement for life, but Neva had seen Janie sitting alone out in the family garden earlier, looking more pensive than usual.

"Did I already tell you about the time Willie collected an entire mason jar of ladybugs, then let them all out in my room while I was sleeping? Mama and Daddy were plucking ladybugs out of the house for at least a year after that."

Breeze and Carly laughed, and Janie smiled.

Or sort of smiled.

Neva was ashamed that she'd discovered a wish on the tree at the square that she was sure was written by Janie.

Love and joy flow with ease to me. As I will it, so it will be.

The wording sounded like poetry, and through her guilt, Neva was quite impressed. It wasn't her fault that she recognized the writing right away. She'd been seeing Janie's flowy cursive all over lists and recipes she was putting into a binder in the kitchen.

While Carly was their creator of food concoctions, Janie had her own skills in creating combinations of ingredients, like the floor wash, that made the house practically dance with glee. She was teaching Neva all about different oils and what they were used for. Like rosemary for an antiseptic and wild orange for a degreaser—a tip she was going to share with Loretta if she ever came back. Then if she remembered right, peppermint could repel bugs and mice and even promote a feeling of peace throughout the house. She needed to get a big bottle of that made up for the next unruly guests and coat their room with it while they were out hiking.

"Tell Mama about the ransom note," Breeze said.

Neva nodded. She'd told Breeze about it when they were weeding the flower bed and the girl had found it hilarious.

"Not much to tell but I still remember the stripes Daddy made on Willie's bare legs with the hickory stick after he finally found me locked in the closet."

Breeze filled in the rest of it, telling how Willie had dyed Neva's hands with red food coloring and then made out a fake ransom note and pretended she'd been kidnapped. Her parents were beside themselves with terror for at least an hour until they heard her kicking at the coat closet door to be let out. Her boot marks were still in there, as Breeze had pointed out shortly after their conversation when she'd gone looking for evidence.

Now Neva watched Janie while Breeze told the

story. Janie was different since their talk in the kitchen about her husband. Hopefully that meant she'd reach out to him soon and let him visit the girls.

"And he made Ms. Cabot believe that she had to eat the paper in fortune cookies for them to come true," Breeze said. "She ate tons of them."

That one made Janie laugh out loud and the sound made Neva's heart smile. She didn't know what it was, but something about Janie touched a part of Neva she hadn't even known she had. It felt, well…maternal.

Or at least what she thought a maternal feeling would be. She wondered about Janie's mom, whether she was still living, but since Janie hadn't mentioned her, Neva didn't want to either.

Suddenly Neva sat upright in her chair, then leaned forward and squinted to see if the form coming up the sidewalk was really who she thought it was.

"Charm, look pretty. Your sweetheart is coming this way."

Not only was Myster sauntering down the side-walk, tail held high as though proudly leading a parade, but behind him was Greta. She carried a small bag and she looked pleased with herself.

"What in the world," Neva said, getting to her feet.

"Hello, Neva," Greta called out. "Once you take these curlers down for me, I'll be ready."

Charm dashed off the porch and went running behind the house, Myster swiftly giving chase, and Neva went down the steps and met Greta.

She guided her up on the porch and noticed that

she did indeed have a few curlers in her hair. They weren't in properly and dangled clumsily, but they were there.

"Greta, where's Henry?"

"Shouldn't he be with you?" Greta looked puzzled. "It's Friday. Aren't we going to Doc's?"

Greta was having an episode.

Friday night at Doc's Fountain shop getting cherry Cokes—and sometimes chocolate Cokes or milkshakes —used to be a routine for them when they were teenagers, followed by a sleepover either at Neva or Greta's house. Doc's was still there but it had changed with the times, now offering juice drinks and healthy smoothies. As far as Neva knew, chocolate and cherry Cokes were no longer on the menu.

"What's going on?" asked Carly.

Janie stood and beckoned to the girls. "Come inside and give Ms. Cabot some time alone with her friend."

Neva passed her phone to Janie as she walked by. "Call Henry Harmon for me, please. Tell him his wife is fine and I'll bring her home later," she whispered, then led Greta to a chair and helped her sit.

"Now tell me what's going on," Neva said. She was going to have to be crafty to get Greta back home and calm her down for bed.

"No, you tell me," Greta said, raising her eyebrows at Neva. "Did he ask you to prom yet?"

Neva felt gut-punched. It was clear that Greta wanted to go back to a time when they were young and crazy about boys. It wasn't surprising. Neva had read that people make the strongest memories between the ages of ten and thirty years old. Not to mention that in her younger years, Greta was quite the rage around town. She could get any boy she wanted, and did so, discarding them one by one when they started to bore her.

Greta's eyes sparkled as she waited for Neva to answer, and it was light she hadn't seen in her friend's eyes in quite a while.

Meet them where they are.

It was so important in patients like Greta.

Yet it still wasn't easy.

"Not yet," Neva whispered.

"Oh, maybe he will tonight," Greta said. "Let's go in and get ready."

"Wait, Greta," Neva said, putting her hand on her arm to stop her from getting up. "I'm not feeling like going out tonight. It's, you know…that time. Maybe we can just stay in tonight. Skip the fountain."

Greta stared at her for a moment.

"Fine. But if we are staying in, I want you to color my hair for me. I want platinum this time. None of that brassy yellow."

Now Neva knew why she'd been drawn to the Clairol aisle at the store the day before and why she'd had to brave the curious look of the cashier when she rang it up, then looked pointedly at Neva's long, gray hair.

"You'll need two boxes," she'd said.

Neva wasn't sure who it was for, but she knew it would only require one.

"Come on, then," Neva said, then led Greta inside.

Neva had played with different colors in Greta's hair back in the day. After the war, it was a time of celebration and that meant color everywhere. Teal couches, pink hair—you name it. But it wasn't like the box of color you could buy today.

Greta bought gold powder to be sprinkled on her hair and sometimes pink or teal swatches to pin or glue in, and later she was the first in their class to have access to colored wigs for a complete transformation.

Neva was the only girl who Greta kept for a friend for long. The rest of them tired of her ways—the bragging, her sharp tongue, and her need to always have her way. But Neva always saw the sadness behind Greta's need to be the center of attention. It was something she didn't get from her own father, so it was only natural that she craved it from everyone else, and especially the different boys she'd been rumored to play a bit of backseat bingo with.

She'd never outgrown it, either.

At the events where they both landed after Greta married Henry, Neva watched as her old friend flirted shamelessly and always had to be the best dressed, with the most expensive clothes and jewelry.

People gossiped about her, saying terrible things like she and Henry had never had children because after all they spent to keep Greta happy, there was nothing left to raise kids. Some claimed to see her playing footsie under the table with legs not attached to her husband. Much of it was probably made up, though, yes, some of it was true.

But they didn't understand Greta like Neva did. They didn't know that she still grieved silently for her only sister—a twin, no less—that Greta lost to the measles when they were only six years old. She'd only talked to Neva about it once and said that when Stella didn't return from the hospital with her parents, it was like being ripped in half and constantly searching for the rest of her body but never finding it. Her parents had not been any help, as they'd suffered their grief in a silent war against one another, making Greta's life harder than it should be.

Neva always thought that Greta was over-the-top because she tried so hard to fill that empty hole inside of herself and wanted a loving family life like Neva had.

They found Janie and the girls sitting in the parlor, talking about a hike they wanted to take up to the falls over the weekend, once the guests were off and doing their own thing.

"Girls, this is Mrs. Harmon, my friend I've been telling you about," Neva said. She tried to be nonchalant, but she hoped that the girls wouldn't ask anything inappropriate.

They greeted her and Greta took a seat near Carly.

"I love your hair," she told her. "I wear mine in a horse tail now and then. You should tie a ribbon on it."

Neva laughed gently. Greta was really on the hair

kick. "She's talking about your ponytail. We used to call them horse tails."

"That makes sense," Janie said.

"Greta, this is Janie and her girls, Carly and Breeze. Remember me telling you about them? Carly has been doing most of the cooking here and Breeze is our all-hands-on-deck girl for whatever we need. Oh, and Janie is filling in for Loretta until she gets back."

"Loretta is such a flake," Greta said.

Neva ignored the barb but noticed she seemed to be back to the present.

"Janie, can you come help me in the kitchen?" she asked. "Greta, I'm going to get you some lemonade. You must be parched."

She quickly left her with the girls and headed to the kitchen.

Janie fell in behind her. "I called Mr. Harmon. He said he'd fallen asleep in his recliner and didn't even know she was gone. He was really upset."

"Poor Henry. Did you tell him I'd bring her home later?"

Janie nodded and handed Neva her phone on her way to the cupboard. She pulled out a glass and filled it with a few cubes of ice, then topped it with lemonade.

They heard a round of giggling.

"We'd better get back in there," Neva said. "Greta can be a bit inappropriate with the younger crowd. She has no filter."

Janie followed with the lemonade and handed it to Greta, then took a seat next to Carly.

Greta had the girls spellbound, regaling them with stories of what life in the fifties was like. They were discussing Elvis and his magic hips and how his music made the girls swoon.

"The girls loved the movie *Grease*," Janie said. "Carly knows the words to every song."

"Mommm..." Carly groaned.

"Were there really Greasers?" Breeze asked.

Greta tilted her head, pausing for a moment. "Well, yes, I guess so. Not that we really called them that. But some of the rebellious boys wore the tight rolled-up jeans and did their hair in a ducktail with lots of pomade. They smoked cigarettes in the bathroom, too."

"Boys still smoke in the school bathrooms," Carly said. "But now they use vapes."

"I don't know what that is," Greta said, looking confused.

"Anyway, those kinds of boys were few and far between in Linden Falls," Neva said. "Most likely you'd see the teens here decked out in their long-sleeved plaid button-downs and Sears dungarees. Or some of the fancier family boys wore their lettered cardigans, ironed slacks, and saddle shoes," Neva said.

"And the girls wore skirts?" Carly asked.

"Yes, and I loved the swing dresses and poodle skirts," Greta said, her voice wistful.

"But remember your poodle bob?" Neva said.

"Jackie Kennedy renamed it a bubble cut," Greta said, laughing. "Yes, I remember it well because it took a hundred and twenty-five curlers to set it after each washing. I'd get a stiff neck sitting so long while you put them in for me."

"It did take forever getting the curls perfect, all to finally sweep them up and put them into a poof on the top of your head. And that was not including all the work it took before that to get your hair to take the Toni perms." Neva laughed at the memory.

With as much time as she'd put into doing Greta's hair for years, she probably could've earned her beauty license. It was fun—though not something she wanted to do forever. Her own hair had always been in a natural, flowing style. She'd not been much on fads and that was still true. She hadn't minded a bit to let her blond hair fade into an all-over gray.

Greta, however, had fought going gray for decades. She'd gone into the city for color specialists once a month, getting Botox while she was there, too. Neva counted all her wrinkles as blessings and let them gather as they pleased.

"Then Linden High banned the sock hops because they said the kids who wouldn't take their shoes off damaged the new gym floor dancing to that devil music, as the teachers called it."

"That would be rock and roll," Neva said, winking at the girls.

Greta continued. "After that, we'd fill my daddy's car to the brim with as many friends as we could and go to a drive-in movie or hang out at the record shop. Oh, and my first boyfriend used to get a few beers and take me to the graveyard to drink them. I lost my virginity there when I was seventeen."

"Greta!" Neva exclaimed.

Both girls busted out laughing and even Janie was trying to cover her smile. Neva was horrified.

"It's okay, Ms. Cabot. Carly and Breeze aren't that sheltered," Janie said. "In this world today, they have to know certain things so they can keep from being put in an awkward position."

"Mercy," said Neva.

Greta laughed uproariously, looking happier than she had in ages. She so loved to be the life of the party and it made Neva feel good to see her joyful.

Suddenly she had an idea.

Quite a brilliant one, to be honest. One that was just what was needed to keep Greta happy and busy for a while and hopefully give her exhausted husband somewhat of a break.

CHAPTER 13

a week later it was time to implement the first stage of Neva's new plan, but it wasn't going so well. Henry had already tried to cancel the meeting because he said Greta wasn't in a mood for socializing, but with some cajoling, he'd finally agreed to bring her.

Janie said she knew just what to do to make things better, so Neva was just going to have to trust her. She paced the floor, but it wasn't needed, because at four o'clock sharp, Henry came walking up the porch steps with Greta on his arm.

Neva opened the door to welcome them both.

"Come in."

Henry stepped back but guided Greta inside.

"I'll be back at five thirty," he said.

Neva wasn't going to push him to stay. This wasn't for him, anyway. It would also do him good to have some time to himself after the week they'd had with Greta.

Speaking of, she wasn't looking as happy as Neva had hoped she'd be to come over. Gone was the excitement Greta had carried the last time she'd arrived, thinking she was a teenager again and ready to go to the soda fountain. Now she looked tired and full of anxiety.

Restless. A bit confused.

When she locked eyes on Neva, her face filled with recognition and she settled a bit, looking visibly more relaxed.

As soon as she closed the door behind Henry, Neva took Greta's arm.

"Come on, we're going back to the carriage house."

Greta looked at her funny. "The carriage house?"

"Yes. Remember Janie and the girls? They stay back there."

It wasn't ringing a bell, Neva could see, but that was okay. She guided her down the hall and into the kitchen.

"What is all this?" Greta asked.

"It's for a guest," Neva said, cutting her off and hustling her out the back door.

"We're going to the storage building?" Greta asked.

Well, she was right. Once upon a time that's all it was.

"Shh…you'll see," Neva said.

At the door of the carriage house, Neva knocked and heard a scurry on the other side. When the door opened, Carly stood there with her hair swept up in a French twist, a beautiful long scarf draped around her middle and tied over her shoulder. Her feet were bare, but her makeup was exquisitely applied. A look across the room at Breeze showed her dressed the same, a literal smaller version of her big sister. Neva hadn't realized how alike they really looked.

They had really listened when Neva told them of the things that Greta loved the most in life. Appearance and presentation were the way to her heart.

Carly held an exquisite long silk scarf and she draped it around Greta's shoulders, then stepped aside.

Neva nearly gasped at the transformation of the room behind her as, from somewhere, Carly produced another scarf and put it around Neva.

She couldn't take her eyes off the room.

While Janie had already made it a beautiful little place before, now it was transformed into a spa-like setting. The lights were dim, but they had hung strings of tiny fairy lights across the ceiling, and candles were lit around the room. A very soft and soothing music played, creating the perfect enhancement for an already nearly flawless setting. In the air was a sweet and spicy scent that Neva didn't recognize but was delicious to her senses.

"Come, Mrs. Harmon, let me take you to your seat," Carly said, taking Greta's arm and leading her to the small couch.

Greta's eyes were huge, taking in everything around her while Carly led her away.

Neva followed and took a seat beside her.

From behind a screen set up to divide the tiny

kitchenette from the rest of the room, Janie emerged, carrying a tray with a kettle and small cups and plates.

If Neva had been surprised a moment before, now she was astonished.

Janie was gorgeous. It wasn't even the way she'd fixed her hair with waves falling around her shoulders and little pinned-up pieces in pin curls. And the makeup was a nice touch, too. There was something else—her face looked more relaxed than Neva had seen. Her eyes sparkled with a twinkle that hadn't been there before.

Serving others must really agree with her.

"It's so lovely in here," Greta said, looking around. "Not how I remember it at all."

"I've got a special treat for you," Janie said, setting the tray down on the small coffee table. She handed each of them a cup.

Neva held it to her nose while Greta cradled hers. "Mmm...what is this?"

She saw Carly slip out the door.

"Golden milk," Janie said. "It's a blend of turmeric, cumin, ginger, and a few other ingredients. Some organic honey for sweetening, too."

"Oh, Henry and I went to India once and had genuine turmeric tea. It's supposed to be good for bodily functions, if you know what I mean," Greta whispered, then took a small sip and beamed up over the brim of her cup.

Breeze giggled.

"It's also good for brain function," Janie said.

"Oh, Lordy, I need that," Greta said, a smile finally appearing across her face. "If it could just restart mine from factory settings, that would be a blessing."

Neva felt victorious. Greta's humor was coming alive.

"Oh, that reminds me," Janie said. "I have a gift for you."

Greta looked thrilled. "For me?"

"Yes. I made it myself." Janie reached behind the sofa pillow and pulled out a small silk pouch and handed it to Greta.

Greta pulled open the drawstring and peeked in, then turned the pouch over and dumped it in her hand.

"What is this?" She held up a leather necklace with a pearly white stone attached as a pendant.

"It's selenite, a healing stone," Janie said. "For as long as time goes back, it has been used to clear confusion and restore mental clarity. You can wear it around your neck or keep it in your pocket."

"And it's pretty!" Breeze said.

Greta looked emotional for a moment, then swallowed hard.

"Thank you, Janie. I'll cherish it," she said, immediately looping it around her neck and settling the stone in the small dent at the base of her neck.

Neva was surprised at how much Greta appeared to be pleased with the obviously inexpensive piece of jewelry. The old Greta wouldn't have even given it a second glance unless she thought it worth thousands, at least.

Greta took another sip of her tea. "Mmm. This is really some good stuff."

Neva tasted her own tea and found it…well, interesting. It had a very earthy taste, a bit spicy, but she also found a slight cinnamon taste to it.

"What was India like?" Breeze asked.

"Loud and chaotic," Greta said. "But only in some places."

"And others?" Neva said.

"Mumbai was nice with a sort of seaside charm," Greta said.

"In one word, how would you describe India?" Janie asked.

Neva had coached them that it might be a day of hard communication for Greta, but so far, she was doing fine.

"Holistic," Greta said, then sipped her tea.

Carly returned, carrying a dish, prompting Breeze to pass out the little plates and forks.

"What is this?" Greta said. "More treats?"

"These are Taiwanese dumplings with ground pork, cilantro, and cabbage," Carly said. She set it on the table, opened the lid, and used a set of tongs to place one dumpling on everyone's plate.

Neva had a weakness for cilantro, and the dumplings smelled so divine that hers barely hit the plate before she transferred it to her mouth. It was so good she closed her eyes in rapture.

Greta took a small nibble of hers, then smiled up at Carly.

"Did you make these?"

Carly nodded proudly.

"Good job! They taste very original."

"Thank you. When Ms. Cabot mentioned Taiwan, this was my first idea."

"I voted for hot pot, but Mama said no," Breeze said.

"Tell us what you remember about Taiwan, Greta," Neva said.

Greta finished her dumpling. "Hmm…it was a long time ago. Like India, it was crowded. I remember we went to Sun Moon Lake, and a friendly girl named Lia took us around. She introduced us to street food, letting us taste steamed buns and fried meat on a stick."

"Eww," mumbled Breeze.

"Okay, I didn't eat the meat on a stick, but my husband did," Greta said, winking at Breeze.

"Did you go to any of the big cities?" Janie asked.

"Oh, yes, we rode the metro around and visited some temples. Drank bubble tea and shopped the many souvenir shops. It was all very exciting, and the people were some of the friendliest I've ever met anywhere."

Janie got up and went to the small kitchen and returned with a platter.

"This is Turkish hummus, with fresh-baked pita bread," she said.

"Oh, I see what's happening here," Greta said. "It's a dinner around the world. And who filled you in on all the places we've traveled? Was it Henry?"

Neva laughed. "Yes, but I knew most of it anyway. You know how people are around here. Your jet-setting around was the talk of the town every time you left us in your dust. Most of us lived vicariously through you and Henry."

Greta smiled as she dipped her bread into the bowl of hummus. "I've lived a lucky life, haven't I?"

"I'm going to be just like you when I grow up," Breeze said.

Greta froze for a second and looked up at Neva. There were tears shimmering in her eyes before she turned to Breeze. "That's sweet, dear girl. Traveling is a great thing to do, but make sure it's not your top priority, or you might miss some of the more important things in life."

"Like what?" Breeze asked.

"Well, like family. And you can have other hobbies that don't involve leaving home, you know," Greta said. "Your sister is interested in cooking. What's your passion?"

Breeze considered for a moment. "Fairy gardens. I want to build a really nice fairy garden."

"Oh, now see, Ms. Cabot also likes miniature things. Don't you, Neva?"

Neva nodded, then guided the conversation into Greta's tour around Turkey, letting her fill in the details of a scenic country where East meets the West, its very exotic history, and the exciting balloon ride she took over the city. When Carly smoothly slipped in with spicy African tuna fish cakes, Greta reminisced about Henry's favorite trip and the now famous-to-them Battle at Kruger when they witnessed a herd of

buffalo trying to protect their calves from two croc-
odile and a pride of lion.

"The baby elephants were the cutest thing you ever
saw," Greta said.

"I've always wanted a baby elephant," Breeze
replied, and they all laughed.

"A baby elephant grows into a massive elephant,"
Janie said. "Then what would you do with it? Hide it
under your bed?"

Breeze grinned at the thought of that.

Time passed quickly and Neva was pleasantly
surprised at how easy it was for Greta to remember her
trips and also to tell about them so eloquently. There
were only a half-dozen times or so that she struggled
for a word she couldn't quite grasp, and one of them
would help her.

Silently, Neva admitted that hearing about the
places that Greta had traveled and the adventures she
and Henry took together made her a bit envious. For
the first time, she found herself wishing she would've
gone out and explored the world a bit more while she
was young enough to enjoy it. Now the thought of
leaving the comfort of her home and Linden Falls
made her feel tired.

"Have you girls seen the Grand Canyon?" Greta
asked during a pause of their questions.

Janie shook her head. "No, they haven't."

"Okay, here's some sage advice from an old lady
who has lived a long time. Go see the sights here, in
your own homeland. I'm thankful I got to travel

around the world, but I neglected to seek out what makes our own country special. I feel guilty for that and a bit like I've missed out on a piece of my own history."

"That makes sense," Janie said. "And we will probably take that advice."

"Niagara Falls, the Statue of Liberty. And Ellis Island! Oh, what history that place holds. So many stories. You should see them all."

"I want to go to Times Square," said Carly.

Greta nodded. "I've been there. It was so exciting. You can just feel the energy all around you. But given the chance, I'd trade it for a hike in Yosemite National Park. Now that I'm old enough to know better, I wish I'd spent more time walking in nature than walking through shops, accumulating things I don't really need."

"You have memories, though," Neva said.

"I do," Greta said softly. "Some I'm not so proud of and some that I'll cherish forever. Henry was a good one. I admit, I wasn't the easiest traveling partner a lot of the time."

Neva could only imagine. She remembered that Greta had also taken a few solo trips, taking off on journeys to *find herself*, as the town rumors had it. Early in their marriage, there was even talk that she'd run off, upset at being pregnant, then returned with no belly in sight.

It probably wasn't even true. Tongues wagging, always trying to create drama. But it was true that

Greta sometimes left Henry home. The few times that Neva saw him about town during her absences, he didn't look too upset. Perhaps it was good for them both to have had the time apart. No one really knew what went on in a person's marriage behind closed doors, but oh, how they liked to ponder it.

Greta yawned, and Carly jumped up.

"It's time for dessert. I'll be right back," she said, then disappeared out the door.

While she was gone, Greta rested, and Neva went to the restroom. On her way back to the couch, Janie passed her and leaned in.

"I talked to Max last night. Just for a little while, but it wasn't terrible."

That lit Neva up, her heart flooding with hope. No wonder Janie looked so refreshed. Nothing could lighten a soul more than the first steps of reconciliation.

"I'm so glad. It's a start, and that's what counts," Neva said.

"I told him we'd come home after Greta's event. But I didn't promise we'd stay."

Some of the joy Neva had felt just an instant before quickly evaporated at the thought of Janie and the girls leaving. She hoped that if they did decide to move back, they would visit Linden Falls often. She wandered back to the couch and sat down.

She could tell that Greta still needed the break, so when Janie joined them again, Neva filled the gap, making conversation about different guests who had stayed at the inn on their trek around the states and their efforts to sample all the different locales.

Then she reminded Greta of some of the extravagant and dazzling events she'd orchestrated, not only for the locals of Linden Falls but for many city dwellers who wanted an old-fashioned Vermont wedding or anniversary party. Greta had hobnobbed with her share of celebrities, too, many of them only revealing their real names once the party was thoroughly planned and had started.

They heard a thump at the door and Breeze jumped up to go open it. Carly came through with a tray and set it down on the coffee table.

"Oh my," Neva exclaimed. The tray was covered in delicate pink rose petals and held five tiny bowls.

"I give you rose petal panna cotta over poached peaches," Carly said.

"Wow," Janie said. "I think this is your tour de force, daughter."

"I helped pick the rose petals," Breeze exclaimed.

"Yes, she did," Carly confirmed. "She also helped whip the egg whites, so if they taste as light and airy as they are supposed to, Breeze had a part in it."

Greta was staring at the bowl Janie placed in front of her, almost like she was afraid to touch it.

"I've had this dish before," she said.

"In Italy," both Carly and Breeze said at the same time, breaking the solemn moment.

"Yes, in Italy. On our fiftieth wedding anniversary, no less," Greta said. She looked up at Carly. "Did you reserve the liquid from cooking the peaches? It would make a great base for a cocktail."

Neva chuckled. Greta would always be the ultimate party planner. "Well, I haven't had it," Neva said. "So, give me the details, Carly."

Carly grinned broadly. "It's really not complicated. Just peaches, honey, and rose petals simmered for twenty minutes, then layered atop panna cotta of gelatin, cream, sugar, and vanilla. Chilled for the last few hours."

"Such cute little custard bowls, too," Janie said.

"They're ramekins, Mom," Carly said.

"Ooh, fancy talk." Janie raised her eyebrows over her spoon, giving Neva a knowing look.

"That reminds me," Neva said. "Have you all heard about that woman named Verity Joseph? She's an award-winning chef from Europe. Living here, in little old Linden Falls. Can you just imagine?"

"What?" Carly exclaimed, then turned to Janie. "I have to meet her. Mom?"

Janie laughed. "We'll have to see what we can do."

Neva got another idea. Verity was just who she needed to talk to next. But she had to pull off one thing at a time.

"Greta, on the subject of Europe, do you want to tell us anything about Italy?" Neva asked. Hearing about the only destination she'd ever dreamed of going wasn't hard anymore. This was Greta's walk down memory lane and whatever would be, would be.

"So many things I remember. The views come to

mind first. Even the view from our private terrace in Rome was astounding. The hotels were some of the best I've ever stayed in. Such luxury," she said.

"Is it one of your top places you've seen?" Carly asked.

"Oh, yes, probably so. I remember that on the way to the airport on our way out, I was singing along to the music on the radio, and both Henry and the driver begged me to keep going. When we got out, the driver popped the cassette out and gave it to us as a gift."

"That's so sweet," Janie said. "Did you listen to it often after that?"

Greta paused. "I'm not sure. I don't remember hearing it again. I wish I knew where it was, though."

"I'm sure we can find it," Neva said. "Henry might know."

Greta shook her head. "I probably threw it out. I never kept anything that didn't have a hefty price tag on it. Henry used to tell me I was throwing away memories when I'd toss our theatre stubs or other small things we'd gathered on our journeys."

The girls didn't say anything. They were probably as shocked as Neva was. Why would someone not want to keep the mementos from such grand adventures?

Greta leaned her head back on the couch and closed her eyes.

Neva reached over and touched her hand. "Are you all right, Greta?"

"I didn't deserve that man," she whispered.

Janie and the girls quietly rose and started clearing the dishes.

"Oh, hush. Yes, you did," Neva said.

Greta's eyes popped open, and she stared deeply into Neva's. "No. I didn't, and you and I both know it."

"Greta—"

Greta grabbed Neva's hand and clutched it. "When I'm gone, I need you to look after him."

"Stop this right now. You still have plenty of time," Neva said, though she didn't believe it. Greta looked so much frailer every day, as though the cancer were eating up her life force at a rate too rapid to measure.

"Promise me," Greta said, her grasp on Neva's wrist tighter.

Neva didn't want to make such a promise. She couldn't. Once Greta was gone, she planned to bury that piece of her life and move on.

Henry would be fine.

Better than fine, probably. She knew of more than a few widows who would happily ensure he was taken care of properly. So yes, she could promise that he'd be okay. Even if she had to put the notice herself out in a widow-seeking-widower column, or whatever they called it these days.

"Okay, yes. I promise," she said.

Greta visibly relaxed and leaned back again. "I also want you to find my wish and show it to Henry. I know you know where it is."

Neva shook her head. Spicy Greta was back.

"I'll find it this week if I have time and it hasn't

turned to dust after all these years. I haven't looked in the oldest binders in decades. But if it's there and readable, I'll give it to you, and you can give it to him yourself."

Greta sat up, her expression instantly somber.

"Will you call Henry, please? This has been a marvelous time and I can't thank you all enough, but I'm ready to go home now."

"In just a minute. First, the girls and I want to ask you for something."

Now that she was ready to go, Greta looked impatiently at her watch.

"We want you to plan a party," Neva started. "A big one."

Greta shook her head. "I can't. I'm too sick. Too tired."

"You won't have to do anything except tell us what to do," Janie said.

"We can do all the work, but Ms. Cabot said you are the best party planner within five hundred miles. We need you to direct us."

Greta narrowed her eyes. "What kind of party?"

Neva knew they had her then.

They spent the next half hour brainstorming preliminary ideas to create the best *Back in Time* party anyone had ever seen. Greta even caved on the idea to hold it in the cafeteria at the senior center so that many of their old friends who lived there could be a part of it. She emphasized that it had to be totally transformed, and she said she looked forward to hearing Janie's ideas on that aspect.

The only thing they didn't agree on was Neva's rule that any cocktails had to be virgin. Greta said that took the fun out of it, but Carly and Janie jumped in and regaled her with ideas how to make them interesting and still delicious.

While they chattered on, Neva stepped away to call Henry, and by the time he arrived, Greta was brimming with ideas, babbling on about everything she would do to make what might be her last project her very best.

Her face looked less drawn, and her eyes sparkled with excitement as she promised to pull her old dresses from the attic to loan out and made plans to rent a jukebox and hang forty-five records and balloons from the ceiling and all kinds of things that Neva couldn't keep up with.

Luckily Breeze had the foresight to take a lot of notes.

Henry finally talked her into wrapping it up, then took Greta's arm to lead her out of the carriage house. The girls rushed her on the front stoop to hug her goodbye.

"We loved your stories, Mrs. Harmon," Breeze exclaimed.

"You girls are too kind," Greta said. "These days my mind feels like somebody emptied the kitchen drawer out on a trampoline. It's a miracle you understood anything I said."

Carly laughed. "We did, and I want to hear more.

Will you help me make a bucket list in order of what I should see first when I'm eighteen?"

Neva caught the look Janie gave her daughter, as though she'd lost her mind thinking she'd be going anywhere alone at eighteen.

While Greta was busy, Henry looked back at Neva. "I don't know what you did in there, but thank you for giving me back my Greta," he whispered.

"My pleasure," Neva said, and she meant it as she watched them walk away together, their image as one in the silhouette of the setting sun.

CHAPTER 14

*B*y silent acknowledgment they all knew that they needed to work fast, and three exhausting weeks later, the beginning hour of the party dawned.

Neva stood at the door of the center, ready to welcome in the first guests. Jack Darby was here, dashing in a rustic hunting jacket and ready to help the ladies from their vehicles.

"Ms. Cabot, if you'd like, I can handle this. I don't want you to get a chill," he said, concern etched in the lines over his brow.

"Oh, Jack. Thank you, but I'm fine. But I do want to make sure you remember to drag your sweetheart out of the kitchen long enough for a dance tonight."

He winked at her. "No worries about me forgetting that. I told Verity to pack her dancing shoes in her chef's bag."

Neva blushed at the wink. He was certainly a charmer.

It was a cool evening, but she'd been working so hard inside that the breeze that swirled around her legs and up the vintage cocktail dress felt cool and refreshing.

It was one of Greta's, a fancy number from circa mid-fifties that fell in soft, midnight-black chiffon waves in a full skirt. Neva loved the deep vee neckline and the gather at her shoulder. It felt intoxicating to wear it, and she could easily see how Greta had cultured such a love for fashion over the years. Her dresses were going to be seen on many of the ladies that evening.

Paige, the daughter of Margot, who owned Town Square Books, bless her tolerant soul, had taken on the task of sorting through them, having them cleaned, then matching them up to anyone who needed one for the event. Irene Olson had used her sewing skills to alter them for free, working long evenings and weekends to make sure they were all ready. Leona had assisted, and her husband, Walt—who had showed up minutes ago in a tuxedo tie peppered with bird prints —along with Jack, had helped the widowed men from the center get their outfits together, even shining all their shoes to make them feel they looked smart.

Neva couldn't wait to see all the different styles, especially from the sixties and seventies. Breeze would get to see them, too, as she was their designated coat clerk. She had been thrilled when Greta picked out a short dress she'd worn ages ago and had it altered to fit Breeze. Carly had picked her own, one a bit too flashy for her age, but Greta had encouraged her that, *If you got it, flaunt it because you only live once.*

Janie had decided to let her wear it, but only within her supervision.

Neva still could barely believe that, only a week prior, Greta had decided to change the entire theme. They'd already had all sorts of arrangements and plans in place to throw a sock hop with poodle skirts and a soda fountain, with a menu that would make a teenager's mouth water.

Then suddenly, Greta insisted it needed to be a candlelit night under the Italian moon, a vintage evening of dinner and dancing.

"I've got the most perfect dresses," she'd said on the frantic call at midnight when Neva had just gotten the rampant thoughts in her head to call it a night and the phone set them off again. "We can use the same red-checkered tablecloths we have coming but set them off with candles placed in old wine bottles. Twinkly lights strung all over like Janie did in the carriage house, and—"

"But Greta, the plans are already in place," Neva tried to tell her.

"I don't care. This is my event and I want a vintage Italian evening."

Neva knew not to even try to argue with her when Greta held that tone, so she waited. The next morning when she sat her down face-to-face at her own table, Greta was still unwavering.

So, dinner and dancing under the Italian moon—or rather, under the senior center cafeteria lights—was set in motion, using superheroine efforts and calling in favors from all over town to have it nailed down before they'd be forced to reschedule.

The cafeteria was transformed beautifully. The twinkling strands of lights were perfect to make it cozy, and the electric fireplaces they rented set it all off in a lovely glow. Soft music, wineglasses, sparkling grape juice, and in the corner, a trio of musicians played a soft, Italian ballad. Luckily, one of them had a mother in the care unit and had volunteered to perform for free.

Calvin, their town reporter, had brought in his old radio-cassette player as a favor to Greta, though she said it was just a backup plan in case the band needed a break.

The ladies from the Winey Widows Book Club had donated dozens of empty wine bottles for the candle centerpieces. It was a bit of a shock to Neva how much they'd drunk, though they claimed they'd been saving them for years.

So many of Linden Falls' locals had stepped up, loving the idea of doing something for their treasured family members, donating all sorts of things. Neva could only imagine how many memories the residents would soon be experiencing, moments brought on by such a drastic change of routine. Many of them hadn't left the center in ages—some of them for years.

Neva and Janie had also grappled with another last-minute change when Greta decided she wanted to scrap the casual Italian table settings for something more elegant. Away went the red-checkered cloths and then Janie scrambled to find enough pristine white, layering them with gold placemats and garnishing with centerpieces cascading grapes, surrounded with baskets of fresh-baked bread from the Cobblestone Bakery.

The result was lovely, to be sure, but Neva was still shocked they'd pulled it off. Or...hopefully. They'd see when the guests were to arrive.

Faith from Aspen Grove had made only one stipulation and that was to have the event completely over by eight o'clock because many of the residents were already in bed by then. But from what Neva had seen, it appeared that everyone was hovering and pacing right outside their rooms, thrilled to be invited to experience something fun and different for a night.

"You ready for this?"

She turned around to find Janie, who looked absolutely breathtaking in her sleeveless deep emerald velvet gown. The color matched her eyes perfectly and was striking against Janie's dark hair.

"I don't know if I am or not. What about you?"

"It will be fine. I'm just glad the artist was able to finish the backdrop. But not a moment to spare because the paint is still wet."

"It's so lovely," Neva said.

Henry had footed the bill for the piece, insisting that it had to be the spectacular scenery of the Tiber River and the hills behind it. Neva couldn't help but imagine him and Greta standing there taking in the scene together in Italy years ago.

"What time are they going to be here?" Janie asked.

Neva knew who she meant. The guest of honor.

"I talked to Greta yesterday morning, and she said she wanted to be fashionably late one more time. So, four thirty or so. That will give us time to get people seated for dinner and make sure it's calmer for her."

"That's a good idea. She's really been pale for the past few days. But I must give it to her, she's hung in there. When I saw her last, she had an episode, though. You were outside and she got really frightened and didn't know where she was. But the second you walked in, she was fine. Something about your presence centers her."

She was right and Neva still didn't understand it.

Janie seemed really worried about Greta. Lately she'd taken a very keen interest in both Greta and Henry, as much or more so than the girls, even.

"What about Carly? Is she going to be okay?" Neva asked. "She's taken on a lot of responsibility tonight."

"She's great. Once the party gets started and everyone has seen her dress, she's going to change into her kitchen clothes and assist. Verity has the meal under control and is loving having Carly as her junior sous-chef. She said she's never seen such talent in a young person before." Janie was so lucky that Verity's new husband, Jack, hadn't whisked her away on another deep-sea fishing excursion, according to her friend, Leona. Meeting and working with her had made Carly's day. Or year! She'd already posted everywhere she could on social media that she was being a sous-chef to an award-winning, Michelin-starred chef.

"I have to agree. Carly's special," Neva said. "Hopefully she'll get that scholarship she's dreaming of and find herself prancing the streets of Paris one day."

Janie cringed. "I can't imagine her going that far without me."

Neva gave her a sympathetic smile. "I'm sure it's hard to let go. It's probably a good thing I didn't have daughters, as I get too attached, and they'd still be living under my roof."

Janie laughed. "You wouldn't say that if you were under ours during one of the many battles that Carly has waged on Breeze when she feels her privacy has been violated. Breeze overheard a conversation with that boy, Jonathan, and has been teasing Carly ever since."

"Oh, that's normal between sisters. They're good girls," Neva said. "The best, actually."

A warm silence fell between them, then they both started to speak at the same time and both stopped short.

"Oh, I'm sorry," Neva said. "You go first."

"No...you."

"I was just going to say that..." Neva began.

Janie held a hand up. "Wait. Let me say this before I lose my courage. I've been deceiving you."

Neva stepped back like someone had punched her. She'd always feared that, as a senior, someone would take advantage of her. But not Janie—she wouldn't. But she was practical.

"Well, you've picked a fine moment for that confession. Will there be more or are you saving it for when the clock strikes midnight?" Neva said. Her mind was already scrambling, wondering what it was that Janie had been doing. Stealing? There wasn't much to steal. And Neva was always happy to share what she had if someone really needed it more than she did.

"I want to tell you now and I'm not going to drag it out," Janie said, then took a deep breath. "I didn't just happen upon Linden Falls when I left home on a soul-searching journey. This was my destination."

"And?" Neva said. She didn't see anything too startling about that.

"Because my father lived here, and I wanted to see it."

"Oh," Neva said. "Who is your father?"

"*Was* my father."

Neva felt something bigger was coming and she braced herself. "Okay, who *was* your father."

"It was Willie. Your brother."

CHAPTER 15

*O*nce they all had left and midday turned into afternoon with shadows crawling across the floor from the window, there was only the cat. Myster looked pointedly at Henry as though asking him a question.

Henry stared back. There were no more tears left in him, but also no words.

She was gone.

Just like that. One minute she was holding his hand, and the next she was talking to the sister she'd lost when they were just kids.

"Stella," Greta had said, her eyes widening as she stared at the corner of the room.

"I can't see her, Greta," Henry had said.

"Of course you can't, dear. She's here for me. Not for you."

Whatever it was or wasn't that Greta saw in her last minutes, Henry was thankful for it because she seemed eager to go and not frightened. If she had drawn her last breath in a state of fear, he couldn't have gone on. He had been by her side and protected her for so very long that letting her take this adventure without him felt wrong.

He'd wanted to ask her to stay. To hold on. But there was no hiding from death when it was determined to come for its reward for the long wait.

It took two hours of staring at the wall before Henry worked up the energy to get out of his chair and shuffle across the room to find his phone. He should've called Neva that morning. She would've wanted to know about Greta immediately, and they both knew the party wasn't for the people at the Aspen Grove care center nearly as much it was for Greta—*her last big thing*, if you will.

And now she wouldn't even get to see all her planning in place.

He felt so tired. A fatigue that lingered down into the deepest recesses of his bones and threatened to never cease.

With the phone in his hand, he went to the doorway of Greta's room and stared in. They'd left it fairly neat, all things considered. Though his wife wasn't a big woman, it was surprising how much skill and manipulation it took to get her out of the bed respectfully, and then the room, through the kitchen, and outside to the waiting van.

He'd asked to ride with them, to see for himself where she'd spend the night and make sure she'd be kept safe and warm, but they urged him not to, and after all, it was one of the promises on the list she'd gone over the night before.

He went to her bed and sat. Her reading glasses were still on the nightstand, waiting to be picked up and perched on her nose. A glass half-empty of water was there, a pink lipstick mark around the rim. There were a few notes there written to different people she wanted to say a final goodbye to. On top was one to Breeze, telling her she was to have Greta's entire miniatures set from the room upstairs. Carly was getting the finest set of pots and pans money could buy, that Greta had barely used but insisted she have. And there were notes to Janie and Neva, but Henry hadn't read them, and since Greta hadn't offered, he wouldn't.

He reached over and turned off the light, trying to extinguish the feeling that she was still around him. For now, it hurt too much.

You told me when you married me that you'd never break a promise, Henry.

Her voice rang out in his head. It wasn't fair. He'd only agreed to her requests because he was hoping being agreeable would stall the inevitable. Did she really expect him to just show up there, on the very day of her death, and pretend that everything was fine?

No. He couldn't do it.

He wouldn't.

She'd picked out his suit and tie days before, and last night she reminded him to put a tissue slip into his pocket. *Wear the brown Oxfords*, she told him, and *part your hair to the side the way I like it.*

What would he do without Greta to tell him what to wear? Or how to get his hair cut? Or to send him running into town for items she declared she needed right then. How would he ever decide when to trim back the rosebushes or when it was safe to plant new flowers?

He turned the sound off on his phone. It wouldn't be long before they started calling, wondering where he and Greta were.

Myster sauntered in and sat back on his haunches, staring at Henry.

"What?"

His gaze was very judgmental.

Unfortunately, he'd been a witness to all of it. He'd heard everything.

"I knew you were going to be a pain in my rear end," Henry said. "She's gone. Go home. I don't need a cat, and if I did, it wouldn't be a scary one like you."

Myster meowed, long and sorrowful. When he stopped, the silence was overwhelmingly loud.

"Yeah…I know. I know. I already miss her, too—" The floodgates opened, and Henry leaned forward, his grief so heavy that he fell onto his knees, his head in his hands as he let the ragged sobs free.

He felt robbed. He wanted more time with her. Life with Greta wasn't always easy, but life without her seemed too mundane to fathom.

Myster curled up next to him on the floor, and

when Henry was spent, the cat was still there, his silent but strong presence a comfort. But also a reminder.

"Fine. I'll go," Henry said to him. "But only because I think you are some sort of supernatural cat that can probably talk to Greta, and I have no doubt you'll tell her if I don't keep my word."

Myster stared at him unflinchingly. It was a challenge.

With that, Henry rose and went to the bathroom for a shower. He wanted to crawl into bed on this hardest night of his life, but as he'd always done, he would do Greta's bidding, one more time.

Just one dance.

That's all he'd promised, and then he could go home.

And sleep.

CHAPTER 16

*N*eva was just about to gather her purse and go looking for Henry and Greta. They were over an hour late and weren't answering their phones.

"Do you want me to serve the main dish?" Janie asked. "Susan Wilbanks asked me what the holdup is, and Margot Duncan broke in and told her to stop being so rude."

"Oh, I'm sure Susan did. And good for Margot." Neva noticed that Susan was already in a sour mood over her daughter's ongoing angst, yet she'd strutted in on her husband's arm like a rooster, wearing her own vintage Travilla gown, a black satin with white-tipped ostrich-feather trim trailing on the ground behind her. As usual, if she wasn't the belle of the ball, she was going to be waiting to point out something that wasn't perfect.

"My goodness, I don't know what to do. I'm so

disappointed. Greta probably had a bad day and doesn't know what is going on. I should've gone over there. The nurse was going to stay over a bit longer, though."

"Ms. Cabot, please stop thinking that. You can't be in two places at once."

Neither of them flinched at the awkward use of the formal name. It wasn't the time or place to discuss that they might be related, and that if it was true, she was Aunt Neva. And Carly and Breeze were family.

It sounded much too farfetched to be a possibility.

Neva had told her to not say another word about it until the next day when they could sit down and really talk. Maybe piece together the details to see if it all added up. Until then, Neva wouldn't get her hopes up.

The dinner party was going well, and the guests had been blown away by the ambiance, the peach caprese, and the butter lettuce salad with lemon vin. They were ready to move on to the next plate, but should they really serve the sausage ragu without Greta? She was the one who'd picked the menu! She'd argued for that sausage even though Neva and Janie both tried to tell her that many of the seniors had stomachs too sensitive for it.

"Let them eat the pasta out of it, then," Greta had said, her stubborn streak still strong.

Neva was saved from making the decision of finishing up the dinner when she looked up and saw Henry walk slowly into the room and she saw his face.

Greta was gone.

Neva knew it as surely as she knew her first name. Henry was dressed to the nines, as anyone would expect him to be as the husband of Linden Falls' most fashionable woman, but he had the look of a lost soul.

Without another word to Janie, Neva crossed the room to go to him.

He watched her coming near and she urged him into the hallway, where no one could see him and start asking questions. Neva could've kicked herself for not putting the pieces together when Eddie Preachers, the county coroner, wasn't with his wife when she arrived.

"Oh, Henry," she said, the tears already falling before she reached his arms.

He held them open, and she walked straight into them. At least sixty years had gone by since she'd been there, but it felt the same.

Warm. Comforting.

"I'm so sorry," she whispered and pulled away. How dare she take his comfort when he was the one with the huge loss? "When did she go?"

"This morning. She made me promise I'd come tonight. In her honor."

Neva looked up at him, searching his face.

He was so dashing. After all these years, he still looked the same to her, but now there was so much vulnerability there, laid out for the world to see. It made her heart hurt for him.

"So, you came. You fulfilled your promise and now you can go home. Did you drive? Jonathon is here with his truck. He dumped the Wilbanks girl and asked

Carly to his prom, so he's here helping her out. I'll have him take you. First let me fix you up a plate. Just wait right—"

"No, Neva. I can't leave yet. That was just the first promise. There were two. I must do them both. If I don't, she won't rest in peace."

Neva sighed. He was torturing himself. Probably in shock, too. But this Henry was the same Henry that was hers so long ago, and if she knew one thing about him, it was that he kept his word.

He wouldn't leave until he'd fulfilled it. Seemed Neva wasn't the only one that Greta was pushing promises on.

"So, tell me what the last one is and let's get it done so we can get you out of here," she said. She was also eager to leave and retreat to the inn, where she could grieve her old friend in her own way.

Tonight would be hers because tomorrow she would need to step up and help Henry with the arrangements. Greta deserved the best memorial they could think up—something grand to match the life she'd lived.

"I have to dance with you," he said, his voice apologetic and solemn.

Neva felt the blood drain from her face.

"No."

Henry took her hand. "I'm so sorry, Neva. I wouldn't make you do this if...if...well, she made me swear."

Neva felt the sweat pooling under her arms and her

hands start to tingle. What would people think? She couldn't dance with Henry with his wife lying dead at the coroner's office, not even in her grave yet!

Suddenly Janie appeared, the girls right behind her.

"What is going on? Where's Greta?" Janie asked.

Neva turned to them. "Girls, I'm sorry."

Janie instantly understood and gave Henry her condolences, even as she gathered her girls under her wings like a mother hen.

Breeze began to cry, and Carly swallowed back tears.

They'd only known her for such a short time, but they'd appreciated her for the fiery spirit she had and the stories she told.

"It's going to be all right," Henry said, consoling the girls.

"We have a problem," Neva said. It was no use drawing out the issue, and she trusted Janie and the girls to help her get out of the predicament. "Greta knew she'd have him over a barrel on her way out and made him promise to come without her and to have one dance with me."

The girls looked astonished, but Janie nodded. "That makes sense."

"What do you mean, it makes sense?" Neva said. "No, it doesn't. Not at all."

Janie sighed, looking guilty. "I wasn't prying, I swear, but I made one of the trunks upstairs into my end table and I emptied it out to make it lighter to carry down. I found the letters."

"The letters?" Henry asked.

Neva felt the heat rise from her chest and crawl up her neck and all the way to the tips of her ears. She wished the floor would open and swallow her up.

Janie reached out and touched her arm. "Please... don't be ashamed. They were beautiful."

"Our letters?" Henry looked at Neva. "You kept them?"

Neva ignored his question and turned to the girls. "The letters were before he married Mrs. Harmon." The last thing she needed was her new nieces to think she'd been exchanging words of love with a married man. If they were really her kinfolk, she wanted to be the best example possible.

Henry was speechless, and Neva couldn't even look at him. But of course she'd kept his letters. What did he think? Just because Greta tricked him into marrying her while Neva was away for the summer didn't mean their many dates and letters and the talks of their future didn't exist.

A future that Greta had lived out and Neva only watched from afar.

She probably should've burned the letters.

"Can we please get this over with?" she said, feeling the pain she'd buried for so many years come flooding to the surface.

Janie looked from her to Henry.

"I know you don't want to dance together in front of all your friends. Just leave the door open and I'll ask the band to play louder. You can dance out here, and when you're done, just go."

Neva was grateful that Janie was there to put things in motion and help her out of her misery as soon as possible.

"That works," Neva said. "Carly, you tell Jonathon to meet Mr. Harmon outside in fifteen minutes and take him home."

Henry didn't argue. He looked as resolved as Neva felt.

Janie and the girls hustled back into the cafeteria, leaving the door wide open as an avalanche of chatter fell out and around them in the hall.

"Let's wait until they start a new song," Henry said. "I want it to be official. From start to finish, so your overbearing cat can't tell me I messed it up."

Neva looked at him, confused, but the sound of the current song faded out and she readied herself.

"Wait, I forgot to give them this," Henry said, reaching into his jacket pocket. He pulled out an old cassette. "Greta said it had to be this song."

The first notes of a new song rang out.

"Too late. They've already started and let's do this," Neva said.

Henry tucked the cassette back into his coat and took her hand as the next notes sounded. The band joined together into an enchanting Italian piece, and they began to dance. When the lead singer sang out the first lyrics, Henry froze.

"What's wrong?" Neva said.

"It can't be."

"Can't be what? Let's dance, Henry. I'm not doing this twice."

Henry took the cassette out of his pocket again and looked at it.

"They're playing 'Amor Mio' by Mina," he said.

"So?"

"It's the song that Greta wanted us to dance to. The one right here. How did they know?"

Neva searched his eyes, though she knew Henry would never lie. Greta hadn't known who was going to be there as the band, as it was a last-minute arrangement that only Neva had known. And they weren't given a playlist.

The band had been playing more than an hour, so why had they chosen this song at this moment, for this dance?

The instant they both made the realization, Henry smiled down at her and tucked the cassette away again. He took her hand and led her around the hallway, his step perfectly in sync with hers as the words of "Amor Mio" floated around them.

"There was one more promise," Henry whispered. "But I didn't want to do it. I can't say the words."

"Go ahead, Henry. You know she's watching."

He hesitated and leaned farther down to be closer to her ear, keeping the appropriate distance between them.

"She said to tell you something."

Neva didn't know what to say. Or, more than that,

what Greta would want to say to her. After Neva had returned from her summer away and learned of the ultimate betrayal, she'd nursed her broken heart alone. The friendship with Greta was done forever.

Or at least until recently. Still, through the last months together, they'd not mentioned what had happened. No one had. Even all those years ago, Neva's mother had asked her how she could just move forward without confronting her best friend over what she'd done. Neva had only one reply.

Mother, things are as they are. We only suffer because we expect them to be different. And from then on, she'd kept her expectations to herself, never letting anyone else get close enough to let her down. Instead, she covered her pain with acts of kindness that she showered on those around her. It was much harder to think of your own discomfort when you were concentrating on making others smile.

That was how it went. Well, except for the time years later when she'd confided in the tree. She'd hung her one and only wish then, at midnight on a night so black she couldn't even see the stars. It was the evening after Henry and Greta had flown off to Italy, the place that Neva had hoped to have a honeymoon one day.

She couldn't help herself back then and allowed just one relapse of sorrow. As she lay under the branches that dipped low as though embracing her in solace, she'd cried her heart out and written a few words.

Wish You Were Here, was all it said.

She'd hung the paper, and the next morning it was

gone, carried off in the wind, along with any more regrets or thoughts of what she was missing and how alone she felt.

She'd put it away. For good.

Now here they were, all these decades later, dancing in the hallway like two lost fools. Both mourning the spitfire who had come between them, brought them back together, and now was gone.

The next few days would be hard.

But the moment was lovely.

It finally ended, but Henry still held her hand.

He looked down at her. "She told me to tell you, *it should've been you.*"

EPILOGUE

*A*lbany, New York, and Linden Falls, Vermont, might as well have been a million miles apart. Or at least that's how it felt when Paige Duncan pulled in front of Town Square Books and shut off her engine. She leaned back in her seat, stretched her arms over her head, and took a deep breath.

A new start.

One foot in front of the other. That's all she had to do for now.

And breathe.

Take one day at a time. That's what her friends and her editor had told her. Don't think about next month or next year. Not even next week.

Just one day.

But even getting through one day at a time in Albany meant being tortured by each lonely night that followed. And she couldn't do it any longer. She had to be where people loved her.

Didn't she?

Or was she simply running from being an adult?

The door of the shop swung open and she saw Neva Cabot leaving with a couple of books under her arm. Paige slunk down in the seat, not ready to talk to any of the townspeople yet. She'd debated stopping by and seeing her brother at the hardware store first, but ultimately, and almost subconsciously, she'd driven straight to the place that had always brought her the most comfort.

Perhaps it was because she knew her mother would be there, waiting with open arms.

Or it could be a combination of needing her mother and wanting to be within the four walls crammed with shelves of books, comfortable chairs, a warm fire, and a world of stories that she could disappear into and had many times over the years.

For disappearing was exactly what she'd felt like doing ever since it had happened. Coming to Linden Falls was her silent cry for help. There, in the cozy corners of the town and enveloped in a place that had always been good to her, was going to be her saving salvation. She hoped that as fall rolled in and the comfort of Linden Falls fell around her like a warm cloak, her muse would return, and she could get started on some new illustrations—find that magic again that always sparked from her hands as though they had a mind of their own.

The door swung open again and Paige saw her mother.

"Paige! You made it! Come on in, sweetheart," Margot called out, still holding the door.

There it was. A sudden rush of comfort and consolation fell over her, just from seeing her mom and hearing her voice. The weight she'd been carrying for months and brought with her along the drive felt lighter already.

Suddenly she knew she'd made the right decision.

Linden Falls was exactly what she needed to put her world right again.

A blur of gold ran out the door and around the car, then looked up at the window. It was Gladys, her tail swishing back and forth in a rapid rush of joy.

Paige couldn't keep the smile from emerging from its deep cocoon and spreading across her face as she climbed out of the car and first knelt and sunk her face into the comforting neck of the dog that was such a staple to Linden Falls. She inhaled that familiar and comforting scent, letting it take her back to other fond memories.

Then she stood and crossed the sidewalk and fell straight into her mother's arms.

There were tears. Lots of them. And words left unsaid as Margot stroked her daughter's hair and rocked her back and forth in the first moments of the healing process that was finally to come.

PAIGE HAS BEEN through quite a journey but has another one before her after she arrives back home to Linden Falls. Find out what the Wishing Tree has in store for her future in WISH AGAIN, the next book in the Wishing Tree series, by Tammy L. Grace.

Don't miss any books in the Wishing Tree series:

★ Don't miss a Wishing Tree book! ★

Book 1: The Wishing Tree – prologue book
Book 2: I Wish.. by Amanda Prowse
Book 3: Wish You Were Here by Kay Bratt
Book 4: Wish Again by Tammy L. Grace
Book 5: Workout Wishes & Valentine Kisses by Barbara Hinske
Book 6: A Parade of Wishes by Camille Di Maio
Book 7: Careful What You Wish by Ashley Farley
Book 8: Gone Wishing by Jessie Newton
Book 9: Wishful Thinking by Kay Bratt
Book 10: Overdue Wishes by Tammy L. Grace
Book 11: A Whole Heap of Wishes by Amanda Prowse
Book 12: Wishes of Home by Barbara Hinske
Book 13: Wishful Witness by Tonya Kappes

WE ALSO INVITE you to join us in our My Book Friends group on Facebook. It's a great place to chat about all things bookish and learn more about our founding authors.

FROM THE AUTHOR

Thank you so much for reading WISH YOU WERE HERE, the third book in THE WISHING TREE SERIES. If you are wondering what happened next in my story, I can tell you this much:

When the Italian dinner party ended, Henry returned home to find Myster on his front steps, where he approached him with a tiny black kitten in his mouth. It was a girl, and of course Henry kept her.

He calls her Mina.

Myster returned home once and for all, but not before swiping a cuff link from the suit that Henry wore to the party. He carried it to Charm, and it earned him a few days of affection.

At this point you are probably wondering if Henry and Neva will rekindle their lost love. What I can tell you for sure is that their friendship is revived. Whether the romance they once had is still there or not, buried under all the years, remains to be seen. And perhaps it's changed now. Love in seniors is a bit different than young love, as it's a deeper yet quieter emotion requiring no loud declarations or dramatic endings. It is seen in the way they treat each other and do things for one another, in the words they don't say and smiles they share that no one else is in on. And sometimes, that is enough.

Henry loved Greta very much, but in a different way than he loved Neva. Is that possible that you can love two people? Yes, I believe that the heart has room for an ocean of love, and I would like to think, in some way, Neva will get her happily ever after. In this story she got part of it, because for many years, she'd wished for family to be around her. With the discovery of her brother's daughter and grandchildren, she now knows what it feels like to have people to call her own. And she has Henry back in her life, a blessing she's missed for many decades.

Janie followed her heart as it led her to Linden Falls to her father's birthplace, and she's thrilled with the way it all turned out, but she still must figure out what to do about the life she left behind. Most importantly, about Max, her husband. She'll have to decide if simply visiting the inn occasionally will be enough or if her heart will refuse to let her leave. I have a feeling that her soul is looking to be set free to follow the path she was born for.

Lastly, the feline lovebirds—*or love cats, as we should call them*—were reunited and remain at each other's beck and call while they navigate their romantic moments and lovers' quarrels in the Wishing Tree Inn.

If you have enjoyed *WISH YOU WERE HERE*, I hope that you'll take the time to post a short review on Amazon, Goodreads, or BookBub. I also have many more books for you to choose from if you'd like to read more of my work. A fan favorite is the By the Sea trilogy, which starts with TRUE TO ME. And if you'd like to sink into a longer series, my TALES OF THE SCAVENGER'S DAUGHTERS has garnered over a quarter of a million readers and is loved by many. If you aren't a series kind of reader, then WISH ME HOME (a stand-alone not related to this series but just so happens to have *wish* in the title) would be good for you to start with, especially if you love dogs. See more works by me at my website: https://kaybratt.com

ABOUT THE AUTHOR

Photo © 2021 Stephanie Crump Photography

Kay Bratt learned to lean on writing while she navigated a tumultuous childhood and then a decade of domestic abuse in adulthood. After working her way through the hard years to come out a survivor and a pursuer of peace, she finally found the courage to use her experiences throughout her novels, most recently *Wish Me Home* and *True to Me*. She lives with the love of her life and a pack of rescue dogs on the banks of Lake Hartwell in Georgia, USA. For more information, visit www.kaybratt.com.